Blizzard's Wake

Blizzard's Wake

PHYLLIS REYNOLDS NAYLOR

SCHOLASTIC INC.

New York Toronto London Auckland Sydney
Mexico City New Delhi Hong Kong Buenos Aires

ISBN 0-439-56975-3

12 11 10 9 8 7 6 5 4 3 2 1   3 4 5 6 7 8/0

Printed in the U.S.A.   40

First Scholastic printing, October 2003

Book design by Russell Gordon

The text for this book is set in Berkeley.

To Heidi Corcoran, my right hand, in appreciation

Acknowledgments

I wish to thank Mary Carol Hoff of Devils Lake, North Dakota, whose family sheltered me during a blizzard; Susan Dingle, of the State Historical Society of North Dakota; Cathy Jensen, Inmate Records Supervisor at the North Dakota State Penetentiary; Dr. Jon Hammersberg, for his guidance on medical matters; my uncle, Wilbur Schield, for his fantastic memories of the forties; and Douglas Ramsey and Larry Skroch, authors of *Looking for Candles in the Window: The Tragic Red River Valley Blizzard of March 15, 1941*, which became the background for my novel.

Preface

❄

In March 1941 a violent winter storm moved down from Canada and into the United States. To be classified as a "severe" blizzard, there must be winds of forty-five miles per hour or more, great density of falling and/or blowing snow, and temperatures of ten degrees Fahrenheit or below. In terms of duration or the amount of snow, the 1941 blizzard may rate only as a minor storm. But when a high-pressure area met with a low-pressure area, and the winds switched from south to north, winds of fifty miles per hour increased to eighty-five miles per hour. In some locations the temperature dropped from thirty-three above zero to seven below in a couple of hours. For those caught out in the blizzard, the change in the wind was described as "sudden as throwing a switch."

The force of the wind created huge snowdrifts, rock hard in places, and the tornado-like gale swept up dirt to mix with the blowing snow, so that some of the frozen victims were found suffocated with dust in their lungs.

Because of the mild weather on March 15, and because the revised forecast of snow and high winds did not reach the newspapers until the evening edition, many people in the Red River valley states of North Dakota and Minnesota were out shopping that Saturday, enjoying weekend activities, with no idea that a killer blizzard was on the way.

One

"Ezekiel Floyd Dexter!"

Even without the "Floyd," the prisoners knew it was Zeke's turn. The slight, sandy-haired man with the pock-marked face and the cigarette scar on his lower lip rose slowly from his bunk and moved toward the door of his cell.

A heavyset guard in his green-and-white uniform came into view. He was holding a large paper bag and stopped outside Zeke's cell. Pushing his glasses up farther on his nose and holding them there with one finger, he studied the list stapled to the top of the sack.

"One hunting jacket, one wool cap, one pair gloves," he read aloud. "One flannel shirt, one pair trousers, one set underwear, one pair socks, one pair work boots, watch, wallet, and seven dollars twenty-three cents." Then, removing his finger, so that the glasses slid back down again, he added, "Anything missing, you tell the captain."

At that, he put his key in the lock, opened the door of the cell, and handed the bag to Zeke.

"You change now, we'll go to the office," he said. He leaned one large hand against the wall in the corridor and crossed his feet, waiting.

There were low murmurs up and down the cell block. The men were not allowed to talk with other prisoners cell to cell, but when a man was being released, a guard sometimes allowed the men their good-byes. And so they began to call out, softly at first, then a little louder:

"Hey, Shorty! You gonna get you a steak dinner tonight?"

"He gonna git hisself a steak dinner and the biggest ice cream sundae this side the Mississippi," came a voice from the far end.

"He gonna get more'n that," said someone else, and the men laughed.

And then, from the other direction, "Don't forget us, now. I'll be out before too long."

"Hey, Buzzard!" someone joked. "He'll be a granddaddy before you're out of here, and that's the truth."

Zeke opened the large sack and, caught up in the aroma, lifted it to his face, inhaling his own scent, shut up in a prison locker for three years, five months, and six days. He had his choice of these—the clothes he had been wearing when he was arrested—or the shirt and trousers in the satchel his brother had brought him when he went before the judge for sentencing. Because it was March, he chose his heavy hunting clothes. Zeke took off his prison uniform and dressed quickly, not so much out of eagerness as because of the cold.

As Zeke was pulling on his boots the guard said, "Lucky

for you it was October when you came, 'cause you go out of here in summer clothes, you're like to freeze to death."

The slight man lacing his work boots—the leather stiff from disuse—did not know how to answer, or whether he should answer at all:

Rule #7: You must approach an officer in a respectful manner. Always salute him before you speak. You must confine your conversation with him strictly to the business at hand. You must not address an officer on matters outside the prison. . . .

So he said nothing. When the guard looked his way again, Zeke was standing beside his bunk holding the empty sack in one hand, jail clothes in the other.

"Just leave 'em on the bunk," the guard said.

Zeke picked up the small satchel at the foot of his bed and followed him out into the corridor.

Now, more out of boredom than friendship, perhaps, other prisoners gathered at the doors of their cells for the leave-taking, some sullen and envious, some smiling.

"So long, cowboy."

"Get you a shot of Jack Daniel's and have one for me."

"You play the horses, Dexter, fourteen's your lucky number."

There were seven locked gates between the cell block and the prison entrance, and Zeke Dexter waited silently beside each one as the guard inserted his key. He had not slept well the night before because his life seemed as uncertain beyond the gates as it had appeared to be three and a half years ago, coming in.

They went to the captain's office, and a pudgy man in uniform opened a folder and took out two sheets of paper.

"You sign these, Zeke, and you're on your way," he said.

"You're putting your name to the fact that we've given you back everything you had on you when you came in. Somebody coming to pick you up?"

"Don't think so," Zeke murmured, reaching for the pen the captain offered.

"No? Didn't tell anyone your good time got you an early release?"

"No, sir. Couldn't reach my brother. He'll find out soon enough. Not much to dance about, I figure," Zeke said. He signed his name below the captain's, and the date next to that.

The captain's smile softened. "You get your life under control, Zeke, you can make something of yourself."

"Yes, sir."

"I'll have a man bring the truck around and give you a ride to the bus station. You're going back to Grand Forks?"

"Nowhere else to go."

"Well, here's bus fare, then." The captain reached into a drawer, took out some bills, and put them in an envelope. Then he came around the desk and handed it to Zeke. He grasped his hand, his other on Zeke's shoulder. "And I'll say to you what I tell every man when he leaves here: 'If I never see you again, it'll mean you've turned yourself around. And if I ever read anything about you in the newspaper, I hope it'll be that you've not only paid your debt to society, but done a little bit more.'"

"Yes, sir." Then, his work boots making unfamiliar noises on the tile floor, his chest warm beneath his long-sleeved underwear, flannel shirt, and heavy hunting jacket, Zeke lumbered out to the front entrance and stood just inside, waiting for the prison truck. His fingers toyed with the shape of the coins inside his pocket. It had been a long time since he'd touched money.

Rule #6: You are not allowed to have any money on your person or in your possession. . . .

Outside, a lone bird flew across the gray North Dakota sky, circled, and came back again before it disappeared. It struck Zeke that now, if he wanted, he could step outside and follow the bird's flight with his eyes. He wasn't confined to the view from one narrow window, where birds appeared for an instant like a dash mark on paper. You could never see where they came from, never tell where they went.

A pickup came around the building and pulled over to the entrance. The elderly driver leaned forward slightly, eyes scanning the front hall.

Zeke turned and took one more look behind him—the captain standing just down the hall, the warden's office to the left, and straight ahead the gate to the cell block from which he'd come.

Rule #35: Cursing our flag, our Country or State, or National Government, or this Institution, is strictly forbidden and if reported will be punished. . . .

Ezekiel Floyd Dexter, age twenty-eight, sentence five years, crime negligent homicide, pushed through the double doors and walked without expression to the passenger side of the truck.

Two

Kate Sterling tried to restrain herself as the school bus passed the stand of poplar trees, then the creek farther on. She had been doing so well. *Don't look, don't look!* she told herself. But just as they had for the past three days, her eyes sought it out—hungrily, it seemed—the charred skeleton of a house set back from the road, the blackened cinder blocks at the base. The remains of a water heater, a bed frame, a door.

It was disturbing, her obsession with it—as though she'd set the fire herself. As the bus drove on by—past the rusty mailbox bearing the name DEXTER—she promised that the next time they passed, she wouldn't look at all, would pretend it had happened to someone she had never heard of in her life.

On the torn leather seat beside her Nancy Barrett chattered on about a spring coat she'd seen at Penney's and the shoes she'd wear if she bought it. On the subject of shoes

6

she added, "Look!" and tucked her skirt behind her legs so Kate could see her feet beneath the seat in front of them.

Kate leaned forward to look at the pair of saddle shoes Nancy had bought the week before. Instead of new white laces, they were sporting long black-and-yellow checked laces that tied in a large bow.

"Oh, you!" Kate said, laughing. Nancy was known for starting fads that soon took over the high school.

"And look!" Nancy added mischievously. She pulled open her jacket. She was already wearing her yellow cardigan sweater backward, with buttons behind—the latest style—but now she sported a necklace that appeared to be the same black-and-yellow shoelaces looped around and around each other, tied in back to make a necklace.

"You're too much!" Kate said, and they laughed together. Nancy continued her description of the spring coat she'd been thinking of buying, but now Kate's attention was somewhere else. As eager as she had been to look out the window before, she did not want to look now. Yet out of the corner of her eye, in the periphery, where trouble begins, she could make out the single cottonwood tree, then the Nortons' barn. . . .

"It's pale blue with a black velvet collar," Nancy was saying, chattering on. But Kate felt the telltale ballooning sensation in her chest, the racing of her pulse. "Well, what do you think?" said Nancy.

"Um . . . I don't know about black on you," Kate said quickly.

"Only the collar, Kate! Weren't you listening?"

The bus made the turn by the Lindstroms' farm, heading toward town, and Kate gave her full attention to an account of the sale at Penney's.

Three

Nothing looked quite the same—a strange feeling to be riding in a pickup, having ridden nowhere at all for the last three years. Zeke sat far to the right, an awkward distance from the driver, who steered with his cap farther down over his eyes than seemed practical. He drove with the easy confidence of one who is intimate with the road, however, because he kept only two fingers on the wheel.

"Supposed to snow some tonight," the man said, talking to the windshield.

"That right?" said Zeke.

"But it won't stick round long if the temperature stays like this," the old man added.

Zeke felt as though he didn't know how to talk to people here on the outside who made conversation about the weather. Weather just wasn't a concern to men who never got out in it much. All he wanted was to be out of the truck and on his own. He wondered if there was a prison insignia on the side. He'd forgotten to notice. NORTH DAKOTA STATE PENITENTIARY, it would say.

"Well, we can use a warm spell about now, I reckon," the driver said. "Thing about winter in the Dakotas is it takes till August to get yourself thawed out."

Zeke's lips formed a small smile, but he made no comment. Turned his head and looked out the window instead. The truck hit a pothole and the old man swore.

When they entered the downtown area and turned on Broadway, the driver asked, "The captain give you your envelope? For your ticket?"

"Yeah."

"Okay, then. Tell you what. I'm goin' to pull in the far side of the station, and you can walk to the door over there. I won't be driving up to the entrance."

Zeke was grateful for that. "Sure," he said.

The pickup pulled in at an angle, ready to make a U-turn. "Here you are," said the driver.

Zeke picked up his satchel and opened the door. "Thanks."

"Good luck to you, now."

With a little nod Zeke got out and closed the truck door. Then he walked toward the Union Bus Depot like any ordinary man would—a man who had spent the last three years milking his cows or minding his store or shoveling coal.

Inside, he was struck by the variety of clothes people were wearing. Blue and brown and red and orange. Short jackets and long coats and caps of every description. Like folks were in costume, almost, after the drabness of prison uniforms. His nose picked up the scent of a woman's perfume, something he hadn't smelled in three and a half years.

He bought his ticket and wondered if he had only imagined it or if the clerk had studied him with a practiced eye. But then when Zeke moved away among the other customers, he saw that he wasn't the only one with a small satchel or a clean shave. He didn't have much color in his face, that was true—not the weather-beaten look of a man who tends his cattle. But not everyone worked outdoors, and as several more people arrived he was no longer the object of interest, just one of the crowd, all waiting for bus number 309 coming from Montana.

Warm in his jacket, he walked to the large soft-drink case beneath one window, opened the heavy lid, and raked through the ice for a Coca-Cola. All that were left were frosty bottles of Orange Crush and the smaller ones of Grapette. He took a Grapette, pried off the cap with the metal opener on the side of the case, then went back to the ticket window and laid his coin on the counter.

He stood against the wall, savoring the tangy sweetness on his tongue. Everyone in the room was going someplace, folks waiting for them, glad to see them when they got there, he was thinking. Dwayne didn't even know he was coming, and Zeke wasn't sure he'd be there to meet him if he did.

Four

It was sauerkraut day in the elementary school, and Jesse Sterling was about the only one in his group who liked the stuff. His friends gleefully dumped their portions onto his tray, taking a piece of his frankfurter in exchange, until Jesse's plate resembled a haystack.

"Hey, Jesse, you must be part German, you love it so much," said a boy at the end of the wooden table.

Unlike the quiet of the morning, when Miss Ames had taught latitude and longitude, the room now rang with talk and laughter, the shuffle of feet, and the clatter of forks and spoons on metal trays. After picking up their lunches in the small kitchen beneath the water pipes in the basement, the girls carried their trays up to their desks, while the boys tended to congregate at the large library tables at the back of the classroom.

"He's a Kraut, all right!" said Roger Blake, and then, looking around for the teacher and realizing she was out of the room, he reached over and pulled a shock of Jesse's dark hair down over his forehead, placing a finger of his other hand horizontally beneath Jesse's nose. "Heil, Hitler!" he brayed, and the others joined in: "Heil, Hitler! Hail to der Fuhrer!"

Jesse just smiled and shoved a forkful of sauerkraut into his mouth, letting it hang out on either side for his friends' approval.

His buddy Sid Green began singing a song his brother had taught him, punctuated with the Bronx cheer, accompanied by spittle. Sid had only one arm, having lost the other in a baling machine. And whenever he sang the word *Heil*, he stuck his left arm out in a Nazi salute, which made the song all the funnier:

> *"Ven Herr Hitler says,*
> *'Salute me or you die,'*
> *Ve vill Heil* (splttt!),
> *Heil* (splttt!) . . ."

Here the other boys joined in: "Right in der Führer's eye!"

Miss Ames, who had been talking to another teacher out in the hall, moved to the doorway and looked in, and the boys immediately bent over their lunches again, their eyes doing the smiling.

Jesse wiped his mouth on the sleeve of his striped polo shirt, then took a large sip of chocolate milk from the straw in his stubby bottle. His cheeks sucked in with the effort. He was thinking how to spend the following day. His father saw patients in town on Saturday afternoons, and Jesse liked to ride in with him if he could. "You guys want to go skating tomorrow?" he asked as he pushed the bottle away.

"Don't you want to go to a movie?" said Sid.

"What's on?" asked Roger.

"We could see *Tom Brown's School Days*."

"Nah," said Jesse.

"Then, we could go to the matinee—*Junior G-Men with the Dead End Kids*," Sid suggested. Jesse and Roger vetoed that one too. So the rink it was, in the big auditorium building.

"It opens at two thirty," Roger said. "Let's meet there."

"Dad can't pick me up again till around six thirty, though," said Jesse, remembering how long those house calls usually took.

"It's okay. You can hang around my house afterward," Sid told him.

Miss Ames led them down to a corner of the gym after lunch for music. She sat at the piano, and instead of the two-part harmony songs, which Jesse hated because somehow—the way the teacher played them, soft and lonesome sounding—they reminded him of his mother, Miss Ames played the patriotic songs she'd taught the class the week before. The boys sang these with enthusiasm:

> "*Anchors aweigh, my boys,*
> *Anchors aweigh . . .*"

The marine anthem was next:

> "*From the Halls of Montezuma,*
> *To the shores of Tripoli . . .*"

Jesse particularly liked the army anthem:

> "*Over hill, over dale,*
> *We have hit the dusty trail,*
> *And those caissons go rolling along . . .*"

The boys had made up their own words to this one, but they couldn't sing it in school: "In and out of my snout, see those boogers run about, as my snot nose goes rolling along . . ." Kate didn't like that song, especially when Jesse sang it at the dinner table.

It was the air force number that everyone liked best, the girls because only they could reach the high notes, the boys for the last two lines:

> "Off we go into the wild blue yonder,
> Climbing high into the sun;
> Here they come, zooming to meet our thunder,
> At 'em, boys, give 'er the gun!
> Down we dive, spouting our flames from under,
> Off with one helluva roar!
> We live in fame or go down in flame. Hey!
> Nothing'll stop the Army Air Corps."

Except that the teacher didn't allow them to say "helluva." They had to sing "terrible" instead.

"You'd think we were at war already," Jesse had said to his father the day Miss Ames introduced the songs to the class.

"It's only a matter of time, Jesse," Doc Sterling had said, patiently turning over their supper of fried potatoes and pork chops in the skillet. "With all the misery we can get ourselves into without half trying, you'd think the human race wouldn't go around looking for ways to make things even harder on themselves."

Five

DRISCOLL, NORTH DAKOTA

A half hour out of Bismarck, Zeke began to perspire inside his hunting jacket. The Northland Greyhound bus grew alternately hot, then cold. He would have preferred a window seat, but he was one of the last to board, so had to be content with what gray road, gray land, and gray sky he could see beyond the blond, unkempt head of the young man slumped against the glass. JAMES, read the tattoo on his hand.

He had no idea how long James had been traveling. For all Zeke knew, the bus might have started in Spokane. The young man—a boy, really, whose cheek was pressed against the window, his eyes closed, mouth agape—had probably been all over the country, while Zeke had never left the state.

The smell of old wool, damp with sweat, forced him into the aisle, where he took off his heavy jacket and stuffed it in the overhead bin. Stupid not to have done that before. The weather was mild for March—above freezing—and he had noticed water on top of the ice as the bus passed a pond. The driver had said there would be a fifteen-minute rest stop at Jamestown, and Zeke had figured he could step out and cool off then. But Jamestown was still an hour and a half away.

His sudden movement stirred his seatmate. James snapped his jaws together, straightened, and made a quick pass at his hair with one hand.

"'Scuse me," he said, lurching to his feet, and went to the toilet compartment at the back of the bus.

When he returned and squeezed past Zeke's legs, he said, "How far you going?"

"Grand Forks. Change at Fargo. How about you?"

"St. Paul," James said. "I went out to visit my sister in Wolf Creek because I'm going to join up when I get back. Figure they're going to draft me anyway. Might as well volunteer and see if I can get in the air force."

Zeke stole a look at James. He hardly seemed old enough to have graduated from high school—couldn't quite imagine him in uniform.

"You got relatives in Grand Forks?" James asked. His voice still had the raspy sound of sleep, and in his wrinkled denim jacket he had the rumpled look of fatigue.

"A brother."

"How long you going to stay?"

"I live there."

"Oh."

The next question, Zeke supposed, would be "So where you been?" and he leaned back against the seat and closed his eyes to discourage conversation. But James didn't ask, and when Zeke opened his eyes again, the young man was looking out the window as the bus pulled into Driscoll. One person got on and took the last remaining seat. No one got off at Driscoll.

"You going to enlist or wait and see if you're drafted?" James asked as the Greyhound pulled out again, making a wide arc where it reentered the road. "This friend of mine, his brother's in the One Hundred Sixty-fourth Infantry Regiment of the North Dakota National Guard, and they were all called up."

"Yeah, I guess it's heating up pretty good over there," Zeke said.

"First peacetime draft in U.S. history," James went on. "That ought to tell you something." Then he asked it again: "You think you'll enlist?"

Sure. Uncle Sam needs all the felons he can get. "Don't think so," said Zeke, eyes straight ahead, his voice a mere murmur now. "Got a deferment."

James studied him. "Oh," he said again. "Well, that's too bad. I mean, but maybe you're lucky."

"Yeah, maybe so," said Zeke.

The next town they came to was Steele. Then there was Dawson, Tappen, and Crystal Springs. Every fifteen minutes, it seemed, the large gray bus turned in at a little corner store or gas station and traded a passenger or two for someone who took his place.

But as dusk closed in, the faces around Zeke grew indistinct, and for the first time in three years, five months, and six days, he felt he could do as he pleased—sleep or not, talk or not, eat or not, leave or not—and he wouldn't lose any good time over it. His mind could not settle on what he wanted to do, however. If he decided not to eat or sleep or talk now, there was nobody much to care. His eyes searched out an occasional light from a farmhouse, winking at him through the dark.

Six

A half inch of heavy, wet snow fell that afternoon. Kate watched it during history class, the large, fuzzy flakes drifting past the window, taking their time, her green eyes fastening on first one flake, then another, and following their course down past the window until they disappeared from view.

As much as she wished winter over, she preferred the snow to the urgency in Mr. Kramer's voice as he discussed the background of the war in Europe: Germany invaded Poland; Britain and France declared war on Germany; Russia invaded Finland; Germany attacked Denmark and Norway; Italy declared war on Britain and France; France surrendered. . . . The whole world, it seemed, had gone mad. To Kate it was like a school-yard brawl, where two boys start scuffling and then everyone piles on, fistfights erupting all over the playground.

"Chances are," Mr. Kramer was saying, "your parents fall into one of three groups: Most Americans want the Allies to win but want the United States to stay out of the war. That's the first group."

He picked up a piece of chalk, and Kate turned from the window and concentrated on the man in the heavy brown sweater at the front of the room. "Then you have a second group called the isolationists." Mr. Kramer wrote that word on the board. "In general, people in this group want the U.S. to stay out of the war at almost any cost, and then you have the interventionists"—he scribbled that word too—"who want the United States to do all in its power to aid the Allies."

Hanging on every statement of historical fact, however, was the implied question *What will happen next?* Maybe that was the whole point of studying history, Kate decided—to figure out what would happen next. To keep the mistakes of the past from . . . She didn't finish the thought.

Mr. Kramer wasn't the only one worried about what would happen next, she had noticed. In the cafeteria whenever she sat next to a table of senior boys, she found them more serious and quiet than the sophomores and juniors. And no matter what their topic of conversation, it always seemed to get back to the draft. They talked of cousins, brothers, an uncle even, who had been drafted.

"He's four-F," they would say, meaning "not qualified for military service." Or, of an uncle in the ministry or a man who ran a large farm, "He's two-A." Mostly they did not talk about "if" they went into the service, they talked about "when." It was assumed.

Tom Harrison, however, was a sophomore like Kate, and

he didn't spend a lot of time thinking about it. "It'll probably be over by the time I'm twenty-one," he had said once.

Now, as he and Kate and Nancy sloshed through the wet snow to the line of buses parked on the circular drive, talk turned to what everyone would do the next day, Saturday. Being March 15, it was also the last filing date for income tax returns, which would probably keep many of their fathers home doing last-minute calculations before the frantic drive to the post office. This meant that the family car would not be available for cruising around. So if they wanted a ride into town, they would have to wait till evening or rely on a relative or neighbor.

What was on everyone's mind, however, was the championship basketball game, their own Central High Maroons against Wahpeton's Wops, to be played in Bismarck. The boys were shouting over their heads as Kate and Nancy ducked into a seat, Kate on the window side now.

"You saw what we did to Fargo!" Tom called out to another member of the team. "Hubbard knows what he's doing."

"Yeah, but the Wops have Marty Engh, remember," called someone else as students continued to climb aboard.

"Not to mention Louie Brewster, Glen Sturdevant, and Dorval Schmit," said a boy at the back.

"But *we* have Tom Harrison!" Kate said playfully, and Tom gave her a little bow.

Comments came shooting out from all directions:

"Did you know Wahpeton arranged for a special train to take their fans to Bismarck tomorrow, band and all?"

"Hey, where's *our* special train?"

"Fat chance."

"You know where *we'll* be tomorrow night at game time! With our ears glued to the radio, that's where!" said Nancy.

"What station?" someone asked.

"KFYF Bismarck," came the answer.

On the leather seat Kate and Nancy sat close together for warmth. Doc Sterling was continually after his daughter to wear trousers of some sort to school during the North Dakota winters, but what could she expect of a father? He knew nothing at all about fashion—what was in and what was out.

Sometimes the school declared a Trouser Week for girls, to encourage them to come to school in slacks or snow pants, and then some of them would, even Kate. But more often than not, the girls arrived at school with legs as red as lobsters between the hems of their skirts and their ankle socks.

"Are you going downtown tomorrow?" Nancy asked Kate.

"Oh, I don't know. Dad sees his town patients on Saturdays, so it's easy to drive me in, but right now he's finishing the income taxes," Kate answered.

"I was going to have you and Fran over to spend the night, but Dad's got the flu, so I guess I can't," Nancy said. "And Fran's folks have company this weekend, so her house is out."

Kate knew this was really a question: Why couldn't the girls come there? And she had no answer because she didn't know it herself. All she knew was that ever since Mother died, there were certain things Kate found she had to avoid to keep the panic away. Panic or sadness or both, she wasn't sure. But being around other girls' mothers was a definite no. And doing things there at the house, things like overnights, which her mother had made extra special, were extremely difficult. She lived through birthdays and holidays because she had to, for Dad and Jesse's sake, but she found them excruciating. She was trying, she was really trying, but she wasn't quite ready yet.

"Well, I've got a ton of homework this weekend," she said lamely.

Tall, thin Nancy, in her circular plaid skirt, didn't say anything for a moment. Just hunched down inside her jacket. But finally she asked, "You're at least going to listen to the game, aren't you?"

"Sure. Unless Roosevelt—"

"He's speaking first, at eight thirty."

"Then, of course I'll be listening."

It was the ride *home* from school that Kate dreaded most. In the mornings the bus was already full by the time it got to her, the Sterlings' house being the farthest out of any on the bus route. ("Can't very well be a country doctor if I'm going to live in town, can I?" Kate's father had said.)

And so, when the bus let out the next-to-the-last student, it was just Kate and the driver. She told herself she would keep her eyes closed the rest of the way home. She would not see the things that made her think the thoughts— thoughts that woke her sometimes in a cold sweat, then sat on her chest till morning.

But the driver did not know her resolve. The short, squat man in the sheepskin jacket didn't know that the road going past the Nortons' barn was where a twenty-four-year-old man who had been drinking since six o'clock went through a stop sign and plowed into the car of two women coming home from choir practice. He did not know that Zeke Dexter, loaded to the gills, hit the passenger side of Mrs. Eggleston's Dodge so hard that it took the Grand Forks City Fire Department two hours to extricate a woman's body.

It's been almost four years, Kate told herself. *Four years!*

After the bus made the turn, just when Kate thought it would be safe to open her eyes and that the cottonwood tree, which still bore marks from the crash, would be far behind them, the driver said, "That was some fire on Tuesday, wasn't it? That house over there? They tell me nobody was home, though. Dwayne—that his name?—was at work over at the power company. Lost everything he owned."

Kate willed herself not to look, but invisible hands seemed to grip her head and turn it sideways. Her eyes settled compulsively on the blackened cinder blocks, the remains of a water heater, the rusty mailbox out by the road . . .

Her jaw set, Kate jerked face-forward again, and the driver's eyes met hers for a moment in the rearview mirror. He went on: "Somebody said two brothers lived there, but one's in the state penitentiary. Got five years."

"And I wish to God he had been in that house when it burned," Kate whispered under her breath. Then wondered if she had made any progress at all.

Seven

FARGO, NORTH DAKOTA

He had bought only a bag of chips at Jamestown, so that by the time the bus reached Fargo, Zeke needed food. He thought of trying to call Dwayne again, but a line had formed at the sandwich counter, and the bus to Grand Forks would be leaving shortly.

An older man, in Western hat and cowboy boots, stood to the left of Zeke in line, both of them watching the lone clerk at the counter laboriously fashioning sandwiches out of meat and cheese, mustard and mayonnaise.

"He takes that long to put two slices of bread together, I wonder how long it would take him to add a pickle," the man said, his gray hair curling down over his leather collar.

Zeke smiled a little. "Shouldn't be all that hard to spread the mustard," he commented.

"You taking the 328 bus?" the older man said, then put out his hand. "Ed Osler, by the way."

Zeke shook it. "Zeke Dexter. Yeah. Heading to Grand Forks."

"I get off at Hillsboro. Should have eaten before I came down to the bus. Where'd you board?"

"Bismarck." Did he only imagine it, Zeke wondered, or was there a moment's pause, a flicker of suspicion in the man's face?

"Oh," said Ed Osler. The line moved forward, and the next customer placed his order.

A new driver stuck his head in the door. "Fifteen minutes, folks. Any of you taking bus 328 should take your food on board and be ready to leave by nine twenty-five."

The lean-faced clerk at the sandwich counter did not move any faster than he had before, even though the people in line shuffled impatiently. Zeke and Ed looked at each other and shook their heads.

"What line of work you in?" Ed asked next. He simply would not stop talking—just went on chip-chip-chipping away at Zeke's past.

"I'm between jobs right now," Zeke murmured, looking straight ahead, but he could tell that the man was studying him, waiting for an answer. "Did radio repair for a while. Small appliance repair. Twine . . ."

The man leaned closer in and lowered his voice. "You ever work for North Dakota Twine and Cordage?" And when Zeke didn't answer, he said, "It's okay. You done a little time and paid your debt, and now you got a right to a fresh start."

Zeke didn't blink. Eyes on the sandwich man. The yellow

of the mustard jar. He shouldn't have mentioned twine. Hadn't realized that, just like the license tag plant at the penitentiary, "twine and cordage" spelled prison to those in the know.

"Five minutes!" the driver called, coming out of the restroom.

"One turkey and cheese," said the woman in front of Zeke to the sandwich man.

"Make that two," said Zeke, reaching in his pocket.

"Make it three," said Ed.

The bus was only three-quarters full this time. When Zeke found the front seat unoccupied, he slid into it and parked himself in the middle to discourage company, his sandwich beside him. He stared motionless out the window when Ed got on, didn't acknowledge the man's momentary pause by his seat, and was relieved when he moved on toward the back of the bus.

The driver made his way down the aisle, collecting tickets and counting passengers. And finally the door swung shut, the lights dimmed, and number 328 pulled out of the depot, heading toward the highway.

With a bottle of Coca-Cola braced between his feet, the sandwich on his lap, and a small packaged blueberry pie in his jacket pocket, Zeke ate slowly, knowing this would be his last meal of the evening.

Sitting alone in the front seat opposite the driver, overlooking the broad expanse of windshield that almost reached the floor, Zeke watched the beam of the headlights illuminate the yellow line down the middle of the highway. As fast as a new stretch of road was exposed, the bus, like a huge harvester, gobbled it up. Highway 81 was as straight as a yardstick. Zeke had the feeling that if the driver could have locked the wheel into position, the bus would have got to Grand Forks by itself, no steering needed.

He had expected he might feel better once he'd eaten, that despite the cramped space allotted for his feet, he might relax enough to doze. But he felt as tense as he had leaving the prison that afternoon, as alone and uncertain as the occasional snowflake that raced topsy-turvy to meet its death on the windshield.

He should have called Dwayne as soon as he knew he was getting early release, Zeke knew. So why hadn't he? He couldn't quite believe it would come off without a hitch, for one thing. One of the prisoners would do something to put the blame on him, the early release would be canceled, and there would be Dwayne—the brother who had visited him only twice in prison—waiting for him in Grand Forks. His life was full of hitches. And when he had known it for a fact, when they told him yesterday to make his arrangements and he'd tried to call his brother, the operator had said the phone was disconnected. Why Dwayne would do that, Zeke didn't know, unless he hadn't paid the bill. When you worked for the power company, though, you were supposed to be on call in case the lines were down. Well, he'd find a ride somehow. Maybe the phone would be working again by the time he got to Grand Forks.

Everyone talked about paying your debt to society and getting a second chance, but Zeke had known from the look on the jury's faces the day the verdict was read that he'd find little mercy in Grand Forks. When a man too drunk to remember kills the wife of the country doctor—

the wife who was coming home from church, yet—forgiveness is in short supply.

Never mind that it was the first time Zeke had ever been in court. Never mind that he had never been arrested before for driving intoxicated. He couldn't even testify on his own behalf because he couldn't remember the accident. One moment he was in a bar drinking, and the next he was being dragged out of his car and the police were going through his pockets, the papers in his wallet. One of the officers swore at him because Zeke had been unhurt.

The bus pulled into Harwood. Someone stepped out of a café and motioned the driver to go on. Without coming to a full stop, the bus turned toward the highway again and rolled on, swallowing up the center strip like it was spaghetti.

Zeke felt sorry for George Sterling and his family, of course. The doctor had been at the Dexter home two or three times when Zeke was growing up, and again when Mrs. Dexter had her fatal heart attack eight months after she'd lost her husband. But it wasn't as though Zeke had *intended* to kill anyone that night, least of all Ann Sterling. And now he'd be about as welcome in Grand Forks as hoof and mouth disease. Zeke and Dwayne, who had never been close, would have even less to say to each other than before.

He'd tried living on his own back when he was twenty. Just packed up the few things he really cared about and took off—bummed around for a while, living in rented rooms—but he never found a job that would pay for much more than the food he put in his stomach. So he came back to the house he'd grown up in, not for the companionship or for the things he'd left behind. There was no other place to go, simple as that.

He thought of the newspaper headlines he'd seen when he stepped off the bus at Fargo: basketball, weather, and war. Especially war.

They should have sent him overseas. Put him in uniform, given him a gun. Only place he knew where if you killed somebody, you got a medal for it.

Eight

There *was* spring in the air, Kate thought as she got off the empty bus and waited for it to turn around in her lane and head back to town. A few occasional snowflakes drifted down out of the sky, like the last few crumbs in a cereal box, announcing the end. She was ready for an end to winter, an end to grieving, and especially an end to remembering words better left unspoken.

The lane stretched a hundred yards from the road up to the house, a two-story white frame country home with black shutters that, from the outside, at least, looked as severe as a Dakota winter. Her bus usually got there before Jesse's, and Kate took her time—her thinking time, as she called it, in her walk up the drive. To her right she passed the large piece of ground her mother had used as her wild-flower patch in summer. Sunflowers, black-eyed Susans, whatever would "take." Each spring Kate's father used to plow it up, and around May, Mother would take the packets of seeds she had ordered through a catalog and scatter them randomly, wherever the wind would go. Sometimes, if the day was warm, she would walk barefoot in the black, fertile soil, her dress and hair blowing in the wind along with the seeds.

Next on Kate's right, up from the wildflower patch, was the plot reserved for Mother's vegetable garden, also plowed in the spring. Mother would decide how much of this ground she thought she could plant, and surround it with green wooden pickets. Then she would take a three-foot-high roll of chicken wire and weave it in and out among the pickets, not bothering to fasten it till she reached the two posts that served as her gate.

"Ann, that fence wouldn't keep out so much as a frog," Doc Sterling teased her once. "Any bunny with half a brain would either hop over or dig a hole underneath." But Mother paid no attention, and each spring the weaving of the chicken wire made spectators of her family and signaled another season of lima beans.

Now Kate had reached the lawn—the lilac bush, the row of forsythia, the flagstone walk that led past the well, the pump, the wooden cover of the cistern, and over to the enclosed back porch of their house. The house and barn were on opposite sides of a large clearing, surrounded by various sheds and lean-tos. But if you were to start on the other side of the driveway at the barn and walk back down the lane to the road, all you would find on that side would be pasture. A rickety windmill and a horse trough about a third of the way down were the only evidence that animals had once grazed on that land.

Doc Sterling had not intended to farm when he bought it. In fact, except for the few acres at the front of the property that he had reserved for his family, he had sold the rest to neighboring farmers. It was their wheat and hay and soybeans Kate could see from the kitchen window in summer under the huge white dome of sky. All he wanted, her father said, was a place his wife could grow vegetables and flowers, and his children could race through the clover and explore the creek.

Every year, as long as Kate could remember, she would look out that kitchen window around March at this little piece of Red River valley waiting, always waiting like her, for spring. The last three springs, however, had been so sad that Kate could hardly bear them. But now she had a plan. She would take on a project of Mother's, she decided— something Mother had never had a chance to finish. And maybe, in the doing of it, she could redeem herself. There seemed nothing left to try.

Doc Sterling set his worn black bag on the chair, hung his coat on a hook behind the door, and let out a soft "oof," his white shirt wrinkled, his tie askew.

It was the evening ritual. If he had been seeing patients here at home, there was no coat to hang. But there was always the "oof." Then, as Kate knew he would, he slowly rotated his head from left to right and right to left, massaged the back of his neck with one broad hand, and sat down at the table.

He sometimes missed eating with Kate and Jesse, and this night Jesse had long since finished his meal and gone upstairs. Even when the doctor had appointments there at the house, they often crowded the dinner hour, so that the opening and closing of doors, the footsteps in the front hall, and the lingering of voices at the doorstep meant that, once again, the doctor's meal had to be covered with a pie pan and placed inside the warming oven.

The huge cast iron stove was ancient, passed down from Kate's grandmother. It rested there in the kitchen on its short, curved legs, with its four round lids over the fire box, the top surface extending out to one side over the porcelain-lined water reservoir.

Kate and her father resembled each other. Jesse had the same dark hair as his mother, the narrow nose, the skin that tanned to an amber brown in summer. But Kate's hair was reddish gold, and in summer her face and arms were covered with freckles, "as speckled as a hen's egg," her father said. Same green eyes as her dad's, same round face. Same hair. Except that the doctor's hair was gray at the temples, and his eyes had creases in the corners.

"So," Doc Sterling said, resting his arms on the table. "How was your day?"

"The usual," Kate said in reply. "All we talk about in Mr. Kramer's class anymore is war." She slid the plate from the oven with a pot holder, lifting the pie-pan cover, and set it on the table. "Be careful. It's hot."

Her father picked up his fork and paused. He gingerly lifted the item on his plate and peered beneath it, silently questioning.

"Supposed to be chicken pie," Kate said, chagrined. "That's the crust."

Doc Sterling smiled a little. "Oh. Thought maybe it was a pancake. I've been working so long I thought maybe it was breakfast time already."

Kate smiled at him and put a dish of applesauce and a pan of green beans on the table, then pulled out a chair to keep him company. "It was a recipe of Mother's," she said. She was practicing now, talking about her mother as though she were a normal part of everyday conversation.

Her father looked pleased and chewed thoughtfully, then swallowed. "Not bad, not bad! Crust needs a little browning, that's all. Then I think you'll have it."

Hagarty, more a young cat now than a kitten, trotted into the kitchen, crouched by Kate's chair, and sprang noiselessly up onto her lap. He began to purr the moment he landed, and kneaded her thighs with his paws as he turned slowly around, making a bed for himself.

"Now, who invited you?" Kate said, smiling as she stroked the velvety gray head and his purr grew even louder. "Who on earth called *you* to the table, I'd like to know, and what makes you think you can paw my leg and get away with it?"

Hagarty licked her hand in answer and then, distracted by the scent of chicken, put one paw on the table and looked toward the chicken pie.

"No!" Kate said firmly. She picked the cat up and held him, paws dangling, in front of her. "You just think you can jump up anywhere you like, you nosy little thing! You just think you own the place!" As she drew him fondly toward her the cat licked her nose, and she laughed aloud. "Got a tongue like sandpaper, too."

Her father watched them from across the table. "I think we picked the best of the litter, don't you? Mrs. Moore said we could return him and choose another if he didn't work out."

"I like him just the way he is, except I wish he'd stayed a

kitten forever," Kate said, cradling him in her arms. "Look how symmetrical his markings are. White on both front paws and another patch right in the middle of his forehead. He's beautiful. And you *know* it, don't you, Hagarty? You think you're king of the roost!"

Jesse came into the kitchen in his pajama bottoms and T-shirt and hoisted himself up on top of the water reservoir, the one sure place he could count on being warm without burning himself. "Can I have a ride to the rink tomorrow night, Dad?" he asked. "I'm going skating with Sid and Roger."

Doc Sterling looked across at Kate. "How about you? I've got that tax form to fill out first, but I'll be making house calls till supper time, I suppose. Wouldn't you like to go into town with us?"

"No, I think I'll stay home and listen for the scores from Bismarck."

Her father studied her thoughtfully. "That's not till evening, Kate. You sure? Don't want to do something with your friends?"

She told him then the plan that she had been thinking about for a week now and hoped she sounded convincing. "What I really want to do tomorrow is start the bridge for Mother. See if I can finish it for her sometime."

"The bridge!" said Jesse.

Ann Sterling had been known for the delicate, fanciful creations she made out of broom straws and toothpicks, which she exhibited and sold at the county fair. In the past there had been a castle, a Ferris wheel, a Victorian house, a ship, and a birdcage, and a few months before she died, she had designed and begun the most difficult of all—a modified replica of the Brooklyn Bridge, with just enough wire and cardboard to support it in the critical places.

"That's quite a job you're taking on, honey," her father said.

"I really want to do it," said Kate.

Doc Sterling reached for the applesauce and heaped some on a piece of buttered bread. "Well then, Jesse, I guess it's just you and me tomorrow. We don't want to disturb the artist in residence."

Kate took the cat up to her room and lay on her back, Hagarty content on her chest. She pulled the spread up over them both so that it formed a cape around the animal's head.

"Little Red Riding Hood," she laughed, and his purr felt like a motor against her rib cage. On the wall beside her bed was a framed photograph of her mother at age ten and her grandmother. They were sitting side by side on the front steps of a house, their arms around each other, heads together, in a fond, crazy pose. For some reason Kate had always loved that photo. Loved the mischief in their eyes, the shared intimacy of mother and daughter. Her eyes drifted back to the ceiling again.

Up here, away from her family, she did not have to pretend. Their minister had told her that everyone grieved in his own way. Some people got their feelings out in a matter of months and went on with their lives. Others required several years. It was normal. It was natural. She shouldn't worry about how long it took to feel like herself again.

What Kate had not told him, however, or her father or brother either, was that it wasn't the grieving that upset her as much as the haunting. A feeling of something left undone.

The first year after Mother died, Kate—like the others—cried a lot. It helped some but did not change her much. The second year she asked her father to plow Mother's wildflower patch, and Kate scattered the seeds barefoot in the deep, dark soil, the same way Mother did. But it wasn't enough.

The third year she laboriously set up the green pickets around Mother's vegetable garden, strung the chicken wire, and planted tomatoes and corn. That helped too, especially when the family enjoyed them at the dinner table. But there was something more.

And so she determined that she was meant to finish the bridge, and difficult as it might be, it would keep her fingers occupied as well as her mind. But a thought remained so insistent, so awful—the thought that had followed her like a shadow wherever she went—that she felt as though she were always running, keeping just one step ahead before it caught up.

The one great certainty in her life was that she would never, ever forgive Zeke Dexter for killing her mother. As sure as the sun rose and the earth spun, she would not, should not, *could* not, forgive him for what he did. And wherever he was right now—lying on his bunk in his cell, sitting in the prison dining room—she hoped he could feel the hate she was beaming his way. The terrible, awful thought that kept coming to her unbidden was that perhaps the haunting would go on and on until Zeke Dexter, too, was dead.

At times she least expected it, like now, when she lay motionless, half asleep, the cat on her chest, the fantasy came creeping into the room, slinking along in the shadows, crawling up the bedpost, and crouching down by her ear. Some night, she imagined, when Zeke got out of prison, she would be steering her father's car along the road by the Nortons' barn. It would be early evening, perhaps, just before dusk, and everyone else would be home having supper. But for some reason Kate would be on her way somewhere in the car. And for some reason Zeke Dexter would be going someplace on foot. The road would be empty except for her and Zeke. She would see him walking up ahead, coming toward her, and he would recognize who she was. She would see the startled look on his face as the car began veering off onto the shoulder, the fear in his eyes as she gunned the motor, and then . . .

Kate sucked in her breath sharply, and Hagarty, who had been dozing, opened the slits of his eyes momentarily, then closed them again.

It would be so easy, Kate told herself. *So terribly, terribly easy.*

Nine

HILLSBORO, NORTH DAKOTA

Zeke had never much been one to plan his life. One day seemed to roll into the next, and as long as he and Dwayne had their parents' home to live in and enough money to keep them in food and coal, they got by. What he'd decided in prison, though, was that he didn't want to sit around having Dwayne gripe about Zeke sponging off him. First thing was to get a job and put some money away. After that, get a used car. And then he could think about moving maybe. Have his own place. He didn't have all that much to move, was never one for accumulating things. Wouldn't want any more than could fit in the backseat of a Buick, and then he could live most anywhere he pleased, anywhere he could find a job.

Now, because of an October night back in 1937, three years and more had been subtracted from his life. Three years, five months, and six days, plus the weeks between his arrest and conviction, of sitting in a concrete cell, bars at the door and window, going to work in a prison twine plant by day and staring at his bunk, his chair, his sink and toilet, in the evenings.

He watched the yellow ribbon in the road make a long, slow turn into Hillsboro. The bus stopped in front of a gas station, and there was a soft hiss of the door as it swung open.

The gray-haired man in the Western hat came bumping down the aisle with his duffel bag and accidentally nudged Zeke's shoulder as he passed. He didn't apologize, didn't say good-bye or good luck. Zeke had not wanted his company and he was returning the favor. Their eyes met briefly as Ed stood outside the window waiting for the driver to retrieve a second bag from the luggage compartment under the bus. But his face was expressionless now, void of hospitality. And Zeke figured that was about what he could expect. Either he had to keep the last few years a secret, or he had to open his past to anyone who wanted a peek. Answer anything they wanted to know, and then where would he be?

He was not ready for that. He had paid his dues, done his time, and was entitled to some of the privileges of citizenship once again. Folks seemed to forget that.

"Be about an hour and ten minutes to Grand Forks, folks," the driver said, springing back on board again. "Next stop, Cummings."

The big bus swung out onto the road again, its passengers, momentarily roused, nodding off again in the darkness that made them all anonymous. Only the thin strip of lighting up by the overhead bins showed the way to the exit. The engine whirred as the driver increased the speed, the windshield wipers flapped at the spatter of sleet against the glass, and Zeke found that he, too, was nodding off, his eyelids growing heavy, his arms limp. His head tipped back, his lips fell open, and he began to snore.

Ten

Jesse sat on his bed with his notebook across his legs and his books spread out over the blanket. With pillows propped behind his back, he tackled his homework, beginning with math, saving only a book report till Sunday. The small record player beside his bed was playing "Chattanooga Choo-Choo."

He usually did his homework at the dining-room table beside Kate, but she decided to start Mother's project tonight. It was scattered all over the dining-room table. Jesse didn't want to get in her way, especially when she seemed interested in something.

He supposed that Mother's death had been harder on Kate because so much of Mom's work fell on her now. Jesse did his share, but he had the lawn to mow in summer, the leaves to rake in the fall, the wood box to fill and snow to shovel in winter. And all through the year he helped his dad deliver medicine to any of the patients who were shut-ins and couldn't get it themselves. Though Dad had Mrs. Carpenter come in once a week to cook a few meals and leave them in the icebox, and Mrs. Kolstad to do the washing, Kate still had much of the cooking and cleaning to do herself. And there always seemed to be a sore place festering somewhere inside her—sadness or anger or both all mixed up together.

His own sadness came and went, and there were times it seemed to corner him and grab him and shake him by the shoulders. But then it moved on and Jesse moved on, while Kate just seemed to be treading water.

"Chattanooga Choo-Choo" was followed by "Woodpecker Song," Jesse's favorite, and after he listened to that, he padded down to the kitchen around ten thirty for a bowl of Wheaties. As he passed through the dining room, he saw Kate hunched over a large tray on the table. On it sat the delicate, half-finished model of the intricate bridge. She looked up and gave him a rueful smile.

"Wow," he said, pausing.

"Mother left the hardest part," Kate explained. "All these broom straws have to be attached from the floor of the bridge to the main suspension cables."

The bridge—strung between a tower at either end—was to have been Ann Sterling's masterpiece. She had designed it and begun the construction as carefully as she might build her own house. Whenever she'd worked on it, the family watched warily from across the room, certain that each added toothpick or broom straw might bring the whole thing spinning down.

Yet Ann Sterling's graceful fingers had placed each straw in exactly the right place with just enough glue to hold it fast, and it was a marvel to all who studied its progress.

Jesse got his cereal, then stood in the doorway watching, holding the bowl in his hands. "Do you think you can do it?" he asked.

"Well, I've attached two broom straws to a cable, and so far they seem to be holding," she answered, slowly removing her fingers. "Almost afraid to breathe!"

"It looks great," said Jesse.

"You've got the fingers for it, I don't," she complained, spreading both hands on the table. "I've got fingers like cigars. You've got Mother's hands."

"I've got her hands but not her patience," said Jesse. "Couldn't do it in a million years." He had some idea of what this meant to his sister, though, because Jesse had his own agenda: to make the basketball team in both junior and senior high school. He played on a sixth-grade team each day over the lunch hour. His teacher had organized it for those long winter days when they couldn't go out for recess, and Jesse had proved himself a talented player. He knew how much his mother had enjoyed watching the high school games. So whenever he was up at the foul line, he had this little ritual: He drew a quick, imaginary *M* on the gym floor, his lucky symbol, before he made the shot. The other boys maintained a respectful silence, some of them knowing about his mother and some thinking it to be a religious sign.

Jesse watched Kate study her mother's diagram, then carefully attach another broom straw. "Where are we going to keep it when you're done?" he asked. "It should go someplace special."

"I was thinking about the cupboard here in the dining

room, behind the glass doors," said Kate. "I'll make room for it beside Mother's good china." In trying to attach the next straw, Kate's fingers dislodged the one beside it and she groaned.

"Why don't you come to the rink with me tomorrow? Do something fun?" Jesse asked.

Kate didn't answer for a moment. "No, I really want to get a good start on this," she said finally, spreading another drop of glue with the applicator. "I'll be listening to the game, though."

"If the president stops talking in time."

"He can't talk all night. They'll at least give us the scores."

"But you could always invite some friends here, Kate. Have your own party."

She smiled up at him. "You worry about me too much, Jesse. But you're a sweetie."

"No," Jesse protested, hating the word. "What I really want is for you to start driving. You could go anywhere you wanted on a Saturday night." And he added, "You could drive me around while you're at it."

Kate sat back and surveyed her work. "And where would that be?"

"Oh, the rink, the high school gym, the soda shop, the movies . . ." His eyes danced mischievously. "Or you could just drive me wherever you go. You go out with boyfriends, and I'll just sit real quiet in the backseat."

This time she laughed out loud. "Dream on," she said. "Dream on."

Eleven

GRAND FORKS

The bus pulled off north Third and into the station one minute late. The overhead lights came on.

"Okay, folks," the driver said. "Those of you getting off here at Grand Forks can get your luggage out on the platform. The rest of you have nine minutes, anybody wants to get out and stretch, use the restroom."

He swung open the door of the bus and hopped down to open the baggage compartment.

Inside the forlorn station a man in a wrinkled shirt studied Zeke from behind the counter. Zeke knew that even if Dwayne's phone were working, he wouldn't try calling him at eleven forty-five at night.

"What time do you close?" he asked the ticket agent.

"Long as the buses keep comin', I'm open," the man in the wrinkled shirt said.

"Any objection to me waiting out the night in a chair over there?"

"What bus you waitin' on?"

"No bus. Had a change of plans, and my ride won't be here till morning."

"Well, you're welcome to a chair, but it can't be all that comfortable, seeing as how you just got off a bus. There's a hotel two blocks away—rooms half price after midnight. Real cheap, and you won't get lice or nothing."

Zeke thought it over as the man gave directions. "Out the door there, turn left, two blocks down, it'll be on the right."

A shower and a bed would feel good, Zeke decided. Why not?

Once in the room, however, he could not sleep. He showered, put on his shorts and undershirt again, and crawled under the covers, but his body seemed restless, wired.

At two thirty he got up, wrapping a blanket around him, and pulled his chair over to the window, looking out onto the street below—the neon sign outside the hotel, the pool hall across the way, the occasional car, the stoplight at the corner, the little restaurant farther on, closed and locked for the night. He used to think of it as his town, but he didn't think like that anymore.

Twelve

✳

Kate was in the mood for music. Jesse had stopped playing his records now in his room across the hall, and her father had fallen asleep in his armchair downstairs. He claimed he got his best sleep in that chair, so Kate let him be, knowing he'd wake about two or three in the morning and get himself to bed. She put down the magazine she'd been reading, put on her pajamas, and turned on her radio.

Someone on KFJM was talking about the war, so she switched to WDAY out of Fargo and got a weather report: "Occasional light snow tonight and again on Saturday, with little change in temperature." Tom Harrison and the basketball team shouldn't have any trouble getting to Bismarck for tomorrow night's game, she thought, and continued fiddling with the dial until she found music. A band was playing "Last Time I Saw Paris." Kate turned off the lamp and lay with one arm resting lightly on her stomach.

She wondered about the person who wrote that song. She had never seen Paris even once. Kate and her mother had had a little game, living as they did in North Dakota, the Sears catalog the closest they got to fashion. When they wanted something they knew was unattainable, they would say, with a laugh, "We'll buy that when we get to Paris." Ann Sterling had had a sense of style, and Kate had only to trust that when something big came along—the senior prom, a bridesmaid's dress, a bridal gown even—Mother would know what to look for and where to buy it. Kate, herself, hadn't the faintest idea.

She thought of the dress she'd worn for a sixth-grade party—a white-dotted Swiss with pink eyelet insets—which Mother had sewn, clearly the prettiest dress there. Kate had loved that dress, but had she ever thanked her mother for it? Had she actually said that she appreciated all the work and time that had gone into those intricate tucks on the bodice? And the perm. It had taken Mother all day to give it to her, yet it turned out much too curly for Kate's taste, and she cried angrily over it, as though Mother should have known. Weeks later, when the curls began to ease, had she ever said something conciliatory, thanking her for the effort?

She threw off the covers suddenly and sat up, like someone arousing herself from a nightmare, and reached for the radio dial. Back on KFJM she got another song, "South of the Border." She lay down again, arms over her forehead.

She was conscious of a light moving slowly across the ceiling and then down the opposite wall, and finally the sound of a car outside, coming to an abrupt stop. Kate listened for the opening of a car door, and this was followed by the cry of a child and a shrill, barking cough.

Kate automatically reached for her robe as someone pounded on the front door. Then she sat at the top of the stairs and watched the rumpled form of her father as he headed down the hall, tucking his shirt in as he went, his other hand smoothing his hair.

"Oh, Dr. Sterling, I'm so sorry to bother you. I didn't even want to waste time calling because Corby's making these horrible sounds. He's only had a mild cold, and he seemed perfectly well when I put him to bed . . ." A woman's panicky voice.

"Bring him in here, Mrs. Daniel. Did you check his temperature?"

"It's a little over one hundred."

Kate leaned her head against the wall. How often she had found her mother here. If Dad needed her in the examining room, he'd call.

The child barked again and cried some more, but the mother sounded even more desperate than he did.

"It's the croup, isn't it? I was terrified he might not be able to breathe. I remember when I was small and my sister had it, and . . ."

Their voices grew fainter as they moved into the examining room.

"Now, let's just sit you right up here, Corby, and let me feel your neck, that's all . . ."

More wails, whimpers . . .

"His breathing's so *noisy*, Doctor!"

"Well, he seems to be getting enough oxygen. I think he sounds a lot worse than he is. Do you own a croup kettle?"

"Yes . . ."

And then Doc Sterling's voice calling up to her: "I think we're all right here, Kate."

"Okay," she said, and went back to bed.

One thing she knew, she could never be a doctor. Helping Dad out when needed was all it took to discover that. On weekday afternoons Nurse Everett assisted him in the office. But the rest of the time he practiced alone. If he wasn't here, he was out making house calls or rounds at the hospital in Grand Forks. His hours had only increased since Mother's death, and Kate knew why. It kept him focused, and when the workday was over at last, he was too exhausted to grieve. Yet even Kate knew that he preferred to sleep in his chair because he dreaded going upstairs to that empty bed, that single pillow, the empty space in the closet where his wife's clothes used to be.

Listening to the child whimpering and coughing below, Kate thought of her mother trapped in the car. Who could say whether she had died instantly or lived on for fifteen or twenty minutes in that mangled body?

"Zeke Dexter, when your time comes, may it be slow and painful," she whispered, even though she'd promised herself that thoughts like those were behind her.

Thirteen

❋

Some time in the night Zeke slept. He hardly remembered leaving the window and crawling back into bed. But at eleven the next morning, with a maid calling, "Housekeeping," outside his door, he discovered himself wrapped in a blanket, lying crossways on the mattress.

He got up and showered again, first because it felt so good—the luxury of a private bathroom. Then he dressed and went downstairs to check out. A second man was on duty, a cigarette behind his ear, and accepted the key with a perfunctory nod, Zeke having paid the night before.

Zeke walked across the street with his satchel to a diner, new since he'd gone to prison, and ordered a bacon-and-cheese omelette and some home fries, washing it down with coffee. He was too warm in his long johns, flannel shirt, and jacket, so he took off his jacket and slung it over one knee.

"How much?" he asked the large man tending the grill—

a man around sixty who seemed to be the only employee there, cook and bottle washer, too.

"Fifteen," the man said, and Zeke put a dime and a nickel on the counter.

"You happen to know anyone hiring in town?" Zeke asked.

"What kind of work you do?" the man questioned, resting one beefy hand on his hip, grease streaking his heavy apron.

"Most anything at all. I'll take what I can get."

"Where'd you work last?"

Zeke chose his words carefully. "Did some radio repair. Clocks, watches. But I can do cars. Was thinking of garage mechanic."

"Well, you got the Shell station up the street, and there's a Cities Service on down. They might could use you, but I think the Shell hired a mechanic not long ago. He's four-F—something to do with his back. What's your status?"

Now he had to be on guard against something else: draft status.

"Same," said Zeke. And when the man's eyes traveled his body, he said, "My feet."

"Well, that restaurant down the street was looking for a dishwasher a while back. Check down there."

"Thanks," said Zeke. But when he got outside and headed toward the restaurant, he walked on by. He knew the owners. The wife had been on his jury. He doubted they would let him through the door, much less in their kitchen.

Fourteen

When Jesse came downstairs on Saturday morning, his father had the *Grand Forks Herald* spread out on the breakfast table. A bold headline read, CENTRAL, WOPS CLASH TONIGHT FOR STATE CLASS-A CAGE TITLE.

"We'll whop 'em, all right!" Jesse said to his dad.

"Sports?" His father handed him the sports page without bothering to look up, and Jesse poured himself a glass of canned juice and settled down to read the story.

When he'd finished, he glanced at the section his dad was reading, with headlines like FRANKLIN ROOSEVELT ADDRESSES NATION TONIGHT ON AID PROGRAM, and YUGOSLAVS STIFFEN ATTITUDE TOWARD GERMANY'S DEMANDS, and GERMANS, BRITISH CONTINUE TO SWAP HEAVY AIR BLOWS.

He studied his father for a moment—the gray hairs at the back of his neck that curled down over his shirt collar, the nick on his chin from his razor, the faint brown age spots just visible on the backs of his hands. Sometimes he seemed so old.

"Do you think they'll come over here, Dad?" Jesse asked finally.

His father stopped reading and looked up. "Who?"

"The Nazis."

"Well, the ocean's pretty wide for that, Jesse."

"How come guys are being drafted and we're not even at war yet?"

"Because the president figures we soon will be, I imagine."

Jesse's lips seemed to stick together as he asked the next question: "Do you . . . think it'll still be going on when I'm twenty-one?"

"I hope to God it's not." Doc Sterling looked over and gave him a reassuring smile. "Right now that's Roosevelt's problem; you and I have to figure out how much we can get done today."

"I already did my homework," Jesse told him. "I can still go to the rink, can't I?"

"Don't see why not." His father tipped his head back and held the newspaper up in front of him, looking for the weather forecast: "'Considerable cloudiness with light snow Saturday and Sunday; colder Sunday,'" he read. "Of course we'll go. I've got to run the income tax forms to the post office, and we've got some medicines to deliver."

Jesse pointed to an ad in the paper. "Valley Motor's having a 'Big Ten Sale,' Dad. Look. 'Free trial usage for ten days.'" He grinned. "Want to drive a new car around for ten days, just to see how it feels?"

His father smiled back. "Better not," he said. "Old Gertie out there might get jealous."

Gertie was the doctor's 1931 Model A Ford, almost a second home to Doc Sterling because he spent so much time in it. In fact, if anyone were to ride in the backseat, he'd first have to push aside all the "necessaries," as the doctor called them—the supplies he carried in case he was waiting for a baby to be born and he needed sleep. In a noisy household he might return to the quiet of his car, fortify himself with a tin of crackers and a jar of cold tea, which he replenished daily, then cover himself with a blanket and get in an hour or two of sleep while the baby was thinking it over. Also in the back of the car was a raincoat, should he have to change a tire in the rain, a box of spare parts, matches, a sweater, and other assorted oddities that had sat around in bags or boxes, some unused and unneeded, for seven or eight years.

He was not a neat man, except when it came to incisions and stitches. Jesse had often heard his sister complain about the way Dad kept his bedroom, with clothes and towels strewn all over, the way he left stacks of unread magazines and journals in teetering piles around his office. She didn't complain to her father, she complained to Jesse, but he figured that if you had to be so precise and careful in one part of your life, maybe it was good to let go a little somewhere else.

"We really *do* need a new car, Dad," Jesse said. "No radio, no heater, and the horn sticks."

"I know, I know," his father said.

"It's dangerous, Dad! Sometimes the horn works and sometimes it doesn't. You might need it quick sometime and nothing happens!"

"Just seems to me that when I think about all I've got to

do every day, Gertie's horn takes second place to most everything," Doc Sterling said. "Now, this afternoon I have to drop my income tax off before I make my house calls, so we'd better leave about one thirty." He winked at Jesse. "And if we take the long way round to the post office and drive by Valley Motors, I don't suppose Gertie will notice, as long as you understand we're just looking."

"All *right*!" Jesse said. Then, hesitating, he asked, "There aren't any babies due, are there?" He was always afraid that when he rode in with his father, and his dad was supposed to pick him up later, there would be a patient in labor and Jesse would be stuck out in the car for five or six hours waiting for the baby to be born.

"Not any of 'em close, but in my business, Jesse, there's always room for surprises," his father said. And then he pushed away from the table and took his dishes to the sink. "Hoped I could get to those limbs out back; we're running low on stove wood. Well, that ax will have to wait till tomorrow, I guess."

Even though there was a coal-burning furnace in the cellar, there was a potbellied stove in the parlor, where patients waited their turn to see the doctor. Early each morning Jesse would hear the *scrape, scrape* of his father's shovel down in the coal bin, and after a while he would feel the heat from the register spreading across his face, warming the air that he breathed. If his father didn't bank the furnace before he went to bed each night, the fire would go out entirely and the house would get so cold that the toilets would freeze over. The big, old house was drafty, so it was Jesse's job to keep the parlor warm for Dad's patients. Every fallen limb, every broken branch on the property, was dragged around near the back porch to await the chopping block.

Jesse opened the door of the icebox and rummaged about among the covered dishes. "Do we have any more of that chocolate pie Mrs. Carpenter made for us?" he asked.

"If we do, one of those pieces has my name on it," his father said. "If I'm going to do any chopping this weekend, I've got to have something to look forward to when I'm done."

Fifteen

There was something about having the house to herself and Hagarty that Kate enjoyed. When her father and brother drove off that afternoon, and she had washed the lunch dishes, she sat at the window with the cat on her lap, watching sparrows feed on the crusts of bread that she had thrown out on the frozen ground.

Mrs. Kolstad was out on the back porch finishing up the laundry. There was no heat on the porch, but the glass windows were steamed up from the water in the wash tubs. Kate watched her feed the last sheet through the wringer. Then Mrs. Kolstad threw on her coat and carried a basket of damp clothes outside, working quickly, the clothespin bag sliding along the line ahead of her, a clothespin in her mouth. As soon as the last clothes were hung and the water emptied, she'd be off in her old Model T. The wind whipped at the sheets on the line, and Kate knew they would be stiff as a board when she brought them in later.

She might even leave them out on the line all night if it didn't snow. Mrs. Kolstad had come late today.

Kate had lived here in the Red River valley her whole fifteen years. She'd been to Bismarck twice, once each to Minneapolis and Chicago, and wasn't sure just where she would prefer to live. Not Chicago, she was certain, with canyons for streets, dwarfed as she had felt by the tall buildings. Possibly Minneapolis. The flat, fertile fields of eastern North Dakota were home to her, however—the roads coming together at perfect right angles.

But life out here in the country could get lonesome at times. They could see no other house from the front stoop. Only road to the right until it disappeared behind the Finleys' walnut grove, and road to the left where it passed potato fields and, some distance away, a neighbor's barn. But everyone knew that if someone fell off a silo or got a foot caught in a mower or woke with a muscle spasm or got the chicken pox, you didn't have to go all the way into Grand Forks, because Doc Sterling lived just a couple miles up the road, and that's the way her father wanted it.

She had worked some more on the bridge that morning and somehow managed to undo all the progress she had made the day before. She'd given up in tears and put it back on the shelf. But now, with a cup of sassafras tea and a warm half-cat–half-kitten on her lap, she felt she might tackle it again if she had the patience.

What puzzled her most about the last three and a half years was how easily, it seemed, Jesse had got over it. The crash. He'd been only seven when it happened, and you'd think it would have been worst of all for him. And sometimes it seemed to be, because Kate would find him lying facedown, his head on his arms, crying from missing his mother. But then, amazingly, it was over. He would put on a record or call up a friend, but for her there were reminders everywhere. Her mother's recipe box on the kitchen counter, her wedding picture in the hall . . . Still, maybe Kate could get to be like Jesse, given time. Maybe she could just have a good long cry, say her good-bye, and get on with things.

The ringing of the telephone—two long rings and one short—caused her to jump, but Hagarty only extended his back in a long, slow, languorous stretch, extending, then retracting, his claws in pleasure.

"Sorry," Kate told him as she picked him up and set him back down on the warmth of her cushion, and finally picked up the phone.

"It's Mrs. Downs, Kate," came a voice in obvious pain. "Is your father there?"

"I'm afraid not. He's gone into town and I doubt he'll be back before eight this evening. Is there anything I can do?" Kate asked.

"Oh, dear, I've done the stupidest thing. A pot holder caught fire on my stove and I tried to get it to the sink. The flames went right over my hand, and it hurts like the dickens."

There were a few things Kate could advise with confidence, having heard her father recite them so often. If she didn't know how to answer, she asked a patient to call Mrs. Everett, hoping that Dad's nurse would be home.

Mrs. Downs answered her next question before she asked. "I tried calling Mrs. Everett, but she's not there. Do I wash the burn before I treat it, or what?"

"When you burn yourself in a direct flame, Mrs. Downs,

the heat usually kills the germs, so all you have to do is bandage it. Do you have any Vaseline?"

"Yes."

"Smear some over the burn, then freshly iron a clean handkerchief and wrap it around your hand."

"I can't just get a handkerchief from the drawer?"

"It really should be sterilized, and it will be if you iron it," Kate explained.

"You're a dear. Thank you so much."

Kate liked to feel needed, and decided to bake something they all could enjoy that night after Roosevelt spoke, or later, while they listened to the game. A yellow sheet cake with brown-sugar icing maybe.

Mrs. Kolstad came in at last around five, her cheeks and hands red. Kate waited for her usual comment about how much faster she could do the wash if they had an Easy Spindrier, like Mrs. Saunders had in town, even though she knew that meant a house wired for electricity. But this time Mrs. Kolstad only said, in her usual dire manner, "Well, that's that for another week. Can't wait for warm weather to get here, when you can hang up the clothes before they half freeze on you."

"That will be a treat," Kate said. "Have a good week, Mrs. Kolstad."

Kate set to work mixing the eggs and shortening and turned the radio to KFJM.

". . . zero visibility," an announcer was saying. Kate glanced out the window. Well, whatever place that forecast was for, it certainly wasn't here. In the gathering dusk she could still see the thermometer outside the kitchen window. It had dropped only two degrees since morning, and everything beyond the window—the fallen limbs in the back-yard, the shed, and the barn—were clearly visible.

She changed stations to WDAY. Later they would broad-cast the *National Barn Dance,* starring Eddie Peabody, and after the president's speech, the NBC orchestra. But Kate would be tuned to Bismarck by then for the game. Right now there was a program called "Defense of America," and Kate turned the radio off.

At six-forty five the phone rang again, and Kate lifted the receiver.

"Any calls, Kate?" her father asked.

"One. Mrs. Downs burned her hand. I told her you wouldn't be back till later and how she should bandage it."

"Severe burn?"

"Flames from a burning potholder. I told her she didn't need to wash it."

"Good. I just picked up Jesse and we're over at the Dryburgs' farm. Mr. Dryburg's got an infection in that toe I treated last month, and it's not looking too good. I'm going to have to work on that, and Mrs. Dryburg's giving us sup-per. So you go on and eat, and we'll be home when we get there."

"You won't miss the president's speech, will you?" Kate asked.

"No, we'll be back by then, the way Jesse's breathing down my neck. Wants to be home in time to listen to the game. But if I'm not there to hear Mr. Roosevelt, you listen for me, okay?"

"All right," Kate agreed. "It's just you and me for supper, Hagarty," she said to the cat as she hung up the phone. "You have your choice of chicken or beans and cornbread. Yeah? Me too. Chicken it is."

Sixteen

There were more people in town than Zeke had expected on a Saturday in March. But the air was so mild for North Dakota you'd almost think it was spring. Lots of people dropping off their tax forms at the post office and stopping to read the advertisements for the Rhythm Aces Band at the Eagle Ballroom and Ken Sutton's Orchestra at the States Ballroom.

It was Local Entertainment Nite at the Dacotah Hotel, and there was a choice of movies in the theaters—*Dr. Kildare Goes Home*, with Lionel Barrymore, or *This Thing Called Love*, with Rosalind Russell. It was an odd feeling to be standing outside a theater looking at a life-size poster of Rosalind Russell, Zeke thought, when all he'd seen of the actress in the last three and a half years was a pinup picture on an inmate's wall.

He was not eager to be recognized. When he'd entered prison, he'd had a mustache and a short, stubby beard, but that was soon remedied. *Rule #32: Every inmate will be compelled to shave and take a bath each week.* . . . He hoped no one would recognize the clean-shaven look, and that by the time they figured out he was back in town, he would already have been hired somewhere and working for a week or two.

Still, two or three people did look at him quizzically as they passed, and Zeke had no doubt that if he turned around, they, too, would have turned to study him some more. Most, however, were simply enjoying a Saturday in Grand Forks, tending to their own business, checking out the Easter hats and spring coats, and heading for JC Penney for the men's clothing sale—TOP COATS $14.75, it said in the window.

Zeke began to relax a little when it appeared he would not have to explain to first one person, then another, that good behavior had got him an early release. Because he knew, as sure as there were teeth in his mouth, that nobody in Grand Forks would associate his name with good behavior ever again.

Even without telling his name, however, Zeke was not having much luck. The draft had not yet taken many men from Grand Forks, and of those jobs left vacant so far, there seemed to be enough older men around to fill them. But some of the merchants could see what lay ahead when the draft speeded up, and one of them said, "Don't have anything at the moment, but you come back in a couple of months, I might be able to use you then." But then he asked the question: "What was your name, now?"

"Zeke."

The man wrote it down on the back of an envelope. "Last name?"

"Dexter."

The man looked up and his eyes met Zeke's. For what seemed like ten or fifteen seconds the man in the blue shirt stared him down, and then he said coldly, "As I said, I don't have anything right now." And he crumpled up the envelope in his hand and threw it under the counter.

Zeke was recognized in the shoe repair shop as well and walked back out again without stating his business. He went in a shop that said, SEWING MACHINES, SALES AND REPAIR, and had got only half a sentence out when the owner dismissed him with a wave of her hand and told him there would be no openings in the foreseeable future.

One place took his name without recognizing it, and Zeke gave them his brother's phone number, then remembered about the phone. What he needed was a car so he could drive out to Central Lumber or Grand Forks Ice and Fuel. Apply at the Marble and Granite Works, maybe.

He tried again to call Dwayne. He found a phone at the Shell station, inserted his coin, then asked the operator to ring the number. And once again, after a pause, she told him that that number was disconnected.

"The whole line down?" he asked.

"No, sir. Just that number," she told him.

Well, it was time he started looking for a ride, he decided, but the fact was, he was hungry. It was going to be surprise enough for Zeke to show up on the doorstep. No sense in showing up hungry as well.

He went back to the diner and ordered the liver and onions for forty cents.

"No luck?" the man said.

"Not much out there, it seems," Zeke said, taking a round stool with a torn leather cover at the counter.

"Well, business ever picks up, I could use you, but right now I don't make enough to pay my own salary, much less anyone else's." The beefy man put a scoop of mashed potatoes on the side of the plate and another spoonful of creamed corn. Zeke paid him and took his plate over to a corner table to eat, facing the wall.

When he had finished, he asked if there were any buses out Route 2.

"Wouldn't have any idea. Ask at the Shell station over there," the owner said, and pushed the grease off his griddle with a metal spatula, dumping it in a tomato juice can near the back.

Still carrying his satchel, Zeke went up the street to the Shell station. Finding the owner busy with a customer buying tires, he stepped into the garage and walked over to a young mechanic bent over the engine of a car.

"Excuse me," said Zeke. "Any buses out Route 2 toward Emerado?"

"Don't know of any. Where you trying to get to?" the mechanic said, straightening up and resting his hands on the frame of the car.

"I live just north of there, near Mekinock. Supposed to call my brother when I got in, but his phone's out of order."

"Well, how big a hurry are you in? I live around there myself, but I don't get off till eight thirty."

"That'd be fine with me."

The mechanic leaned over his work again, his arms smeared with grease. "Me and the wife moved in with her folks 'bout a month ago, till we can get a place of our own. Came over from Montana. Got our first kid, and my wife wants to raise him near her parents."

"You must be the new mechanic."

"That's right. I'll be glad to take you as far as Emerado, but it's our son's first birthday, and the family's having a little party for him—trying to keep him up past his bedtime till I get home." He grinned. "I told 'em I'd drive like the devil with the wind at his back, but my wife—she called a little while ago—says he's gettin' cranky. It weren't for that, I'd drive you all the way, but bein' his first birthday and all . . ."

"I've walked a whole lot farther'n that," Zeke said. "Would walk from here right now if I'd got an earlier start."

"Come back around eight fifteen. The minute the boss says I can go, I'm gone."

"Thanks."

"Fred's the name," the mechanic said. "What's yours?"

"Floyd," Zeke said, giving his middle name. If they were near neighbors, it wouldn't pay to say Zeke. "Thanks again. I'll see you later."

Seventeen

❄

Jesse sat impatiently on the old velvet couch in the Dryburgs' parlor, away from the old man's smell. Mr. Dryburg was diabetic and had an infected toe, turning to gangrene. Doc Sterling was trimming the diseased skin and trying to stem the infection.

A pile of old newspapers sat beside the couch, and Jesse found last Sunday's comics. He amused himself with *Li'l Abner, Henry, Dick Tracy,* and *The Gumps,* but then he heard the clock in the hall chime eight o'clock. He was going to miss the pregame comments if Dad didn't hurry. He hoped the game wouldn't start until after the president's speech. Fay Brown had announced the championship game for the last eleven years, and he would be doing the play-by-play analysis.

Jesse got up and walked to the door of the bedroom where the heavy man was propped up on the bed, one leg over the side, his foot resting in a basin. Jesse's father was trimming the decayed tissue with a pair of surgical scissors, but it didn't seem to hurt the man much.

Doc Sterling sensed that his son was there. "Almost done, Jesse," he said. "Won't be long."

"The game, Dad!" Jesse pleaded in a small voice, knowing even as he said it how selfish it must sound.

"You can help by getting my coat and putting some of these things back in my bag," his father said as he put the scissors down and reached for his ointment and gauze.

What Jesse wanted was for Mrs. Dryburg to turn on their big Motorola in the parlor so he could tune in to the pre-game, but that would have been rude—Mr. Dryburg sitting there in the bedroom worried about his foot, and Jesse listening to basketball stuff.

When Doc Sterling stood up at last, it was ten minutes past the hour, and there was still a twenty-five minute drive home. The Dryburgs lived up near Johnstown, and Jesse wondered why his father couldn't have seen to old Mr. Dryburg while Jesse was skating at the rink. Then he realized his Dad had been seeing to folks south of Grand Forks during that time. Could hardly be two places at once. Boy, if he were Kate, he'd be out in the car every night, going places. He could drive the car around while his father was inside making house calls. He couldn't figure what was holding her back.

He stood at the open front door, moving sideways out onto the porch. A step at a time as his father gave further instructions to Mrs. Dryburg.

"Thanks for the dinner!" Jesse called, interrupting, to hurry his dad along.

"Oh, don't mention it," the red-cheeked woman told him, her round face breaking into a smile for Jesse's benefit.

And then, to Doc Sterling, "I didn't realize Frank's toe was so bad. He's managed to keep it hidden from me."

Couldn't she *smell* it? Jesse wondered. Maybe when you got to be old, your nose didn't work anymore.

"Need to check it regularly, twice a day," Doc Sterling instructed.

"Dad . . . ," Jesse urged from out on the driveway.

Finally they were in the car, the Model A headed for home. And yet it wasn't.

"I'm sorry about this, Jesse, but I've got one more stop to make."

"Dad!"

"It's only medicine. You can run it up to the door yourself. Sadie's sister lives with her, and she'll come to the door."

Jesse's shoulders slumped in resignation. "See, Dad? If we had a car with a radio, we could be listening as we rode. You wouldn't even miss the president's speech!"

"Well, you've got a point there. I'll take that under consideration," his father said.

Jesse sighed and leaned his head back against the seat. Okay, he'd had a good time with the guys at the rink, and maybe that was all the fun he could count on tonight. They'd formed a line, like a long snake, holding on to one another's waists, and whipped around the floor so that the last couple of fellas in line went flying off the end. The trick was to see how long you could hold on, and Jesse had held on the longest. He smiled at the memory. They always let Sid be the leader, of course—because of his arm.

Still, he would rather have been in Bismarck watching the basketball game. He loved sports, any sport, but basketball was his favorite. That and baseball, maybe. He'd like to play forward on the Central High basketball team, but his real dream was to play for the Chicago Bulls. Dad's dream, he guessed, was to see how many of the babies he'd delivered grew up to be healthy adults; Mom's had been to enter *The Bridge* at the county fair and win a blue ribbon. And Kate's? He truly did not know his sister's deepest wish. If she had one, she kept it to herself.

It was eight twenty-five when they got to Manvel and pulled up in front of the old white house where the Morrison sisters lived. Jesse had to ring twice before anyone came. The front rooms were dark, but finally a light came on from an open door down the hall, and an elderly woman in a housecoat fumbled with the lock. A lot of folks seemed to use their kitchen as their sitting room in winter, Jesse decided.

It took a minute for the woman to get the door open, and Jesse tried to head off a long conversation.

"Here you go," he said. "We're sort of in a hurry. Hope everything's okay."

"That's all right," the sister said. "Sadie's holding up pretty good. Doc Sterling's got a heart of gold, coming all the way out here with Sadie's pills. You tell him I said so, hear?"

Jesse nodded and went back down the steps. Out by the curb Gertie looked as though she were falling asleep. Some time ago, a curved piece of metal had slipped down inside one of the headlights, blocking the top half of the beam, so that at night the Model A gave the appearance of having one eye half closed. Or perhaps the old car was winking at him. Jesse and his sister could always spot their Dad's car coming home at night because of that left headlight.

"You're going to miss Roosevelt's speech," Jesse said, climbing back inside.

"Well, Kate will have to do my listening for me, I guess. It'll be in the papers anyway."

Jesse was quiet now. He'd just have to look forward to getting the game as soon as the president's address was over. He and Kate could make some popcorn and eat it in front of the big Atwater Kent radio in the parlor.

"I'm glad you got her that kitten, Dad," he said.

"What?"

"The kitten. The cat. I'm glad Kate's got Hagarty. Maybe it'll help her . . . you know . . . get back to like she was."

Doc Sterling didn't respond for a moment. "What do you mean?" he asked finally.

Jesse glanced over at him. "Just all wrapped up in her feelings. Like she can't let it go—what happened to Mom."

"That's exactly what it is, Jesse. She can't let go," his dad said.

Quietly they watched the road in front of them, where large white snowflakes were floating down now, dancing in front of the headlights before meeting the windshield head-on.

"She can't let go," Doc Sterling said again, and this time they rode several miles in silence.

Eighteen

Kate glanced at the clock at 8:13. If Dad didn't get here soon, he'd miss the president's speech. The yellow cake she had baked sat waiting on the kitchen table, its brown-sugar frosting glistening in the light of the dimming bulb overhead. She'd have to remind Dad to crank the Delco this weekend. Like most of the rural homes, theirs did not have electric lines out to the house, only a phone line. But her father had installed a Delco generator in the cellar with thirty batteries in it. He would go down and crank it once or twice a week to recharge the batteries, and it would make just enough electricity for the radios, the record players, and a few well-placed lightbulbs around the house. Where there was no bulb, there was a kerosene lamp.

As for water, there was a deep well beside the house, and three pressure pumps, one in the yard, one on the back porch, and one at the kitchen sink. Kate was so used to pumping the handle when she needed water for cooking or cleaning that she didn't even think about it. The toilet and tub upstairs and the lavatory off her father's examining room had water storage tanks above them, and a pump jack operated by a gasoline motor filled them as required.

There was also a cistern out in the yard—a large underground tank with a pipe leading down from the roof, so that whenever it rained, the water was saved in the cistern. In the summer Kate would open the little trap door in the wooden cover and lower their milk and butter and eggs in buckets to cool in the cold, clear water. Ice came from a neighbor who had built himself a cave in a small hill. During the winter he stocked it with large blocks of ice packed in straw, then sold it year-round to the neighbors for their iceboxes.

Kate knew that most of the houses in town had electric lines from the city and did not need generators. She knew too that they had city water, and some even had electric stoves and refrigerators. But she did not mind. Like her father, she liked the openness and quiet of the country. As long as she had the radio and telephone, she could survive.

She had been listening to *National Barn Dance* on WDAY. Then she realized she was missing the pregame comments. In turning the dial for the Bismarck station, she happened upon a weather advisory on Grand Fork's KFJM: ". . . interrupt this program for a weather advisory. The weather bureau forecasts snow tonight and strong winds approaching forty to fifty miles per hour, with falling temperatures and low to zero visibility. We repeat: Snow tonight . . ."

"Well, that laundry's got to come in, dry or not," Kate said aloud, and went to the back door. Large flakes were coming down, but she could still just make out the clothesline and the shape of the shed beyond. The storm was obviously some distance off, and Dad and Jesse would get here long before it came. Still . . .

She went to the telephone and asked the operator to ring the Dryburgs'. When Mrs. Dryburg answered, Kate said, "I just heard about a storm coming up and wondered if Dad and Jesse are on their way."

"They left here not more than a few minutes ago, dear," Mrs. Dryburg told her. "Don't you worry. They'll be along."

"Thanks," Kate said, relieved, and hung up. She threw on her coat and gloves and, taking a laundry basket and the clothespin bag, went outside and hurriedly took the clothes off the line, dropping the pins in the bag. The sheets, dry and stiff, cracked like paper as she thrust them down in the basket, not bothering to fold them yet, while the towels, still damp, went in on top of them.

Maybe she should get more wood for the wood box while she was out here, she thought. She took the laundry inside, lit a kerosene lantern to set on the back steps while she worked, and began. When she had brought in all that would fit in the box in the parlor, she piled more on the back porch. Then, as she had often seen her mother do, she set the lamp in the kitchen window near the door to help her father find his way inside after he parked the car. Kate hung up her jacket, then sat down with Hagarty, teasing him with a piece of string from her sweater pocket.

Suddenly she realized that Roosevelt was speaking. The talk had already begun, and her father had asked her to listen. How she was supposed to remember everything he said, she didn't know. She'd already missed five minutes.

She turned up the volume on the radio because of all the static and folded clothes as she listened. It was Roosevelt's voice, all right. "Nazi forces are not seeking mere modifications in colonial maps or in minor European boundaries. They openly seek the destruction of all elective systems of government on every continent—including our own; they seek to establish systems of government based on the regimentation of all human beings by a handful of individual rulers who have seized power by force. . . ."

This sounded too scary to listen to alone, and Kate wished that her father were here. Even listening with Jesse would be better than sharing such news with a kitten. She went to the front door and peered out to see if any car was coming down the road. Then she walked to the back door to see if possibly they had come in and parked and she'd missed it. She stepped outside to check the weather. The snow was coming down harder now. When she returned to the parlor, she turned the rocker so that if any car was coming, she'd see the headlights far off.

"But now the time element is of supreme importance. Every plane, every other instrument of war, old and new, which we can spare now, we will send overseas. . . ."

Kate went to the phone and asked the operator to get the Dryburgs once more.

"They still aren't home," she said. "I was just wondering—did he mention anyone else he was going to see? I thought maybe he had other stops to make."

"Well, now, I don't think so, dear. I know that Jesse was eager to get home. But . . . wait, now. I believe I did notice a bottle of pills with Sadie Morrison's name on it when he was taking things from his bag. I'll bet he stopped in Manvel on the way home to drop those off. Why, that's just what he did. I imagine if you look out your window, you'll see him coming any minute now."

"Okay, thanks," Kate said, and hung up.

But her heart was beginning to pound. She laid out a map of the Grand Forks area in her mind, the distance from the Dryburgs' to Sadie Morrison's in Manvel. . . . Suddenly she lifted the receiver again and rang the operator, asking to be connected to Sadie Morrison, but was told the Morrisons had no phone.

"We shall have to make sacrifices—every one of us," Roosevelt went on. "The final extent of those sacrifices will depend upon the speed with which we act now.

"I must tell you tonight in plain language what this undertaking means to you—to your daily life.

"Whether you are in the armed services; whether you are a steel worker or a stevedore; a machinist or a housewife; a farmer or a banker; a storekeeper or a manufacturer—to all of you it will mean sacrifice in behalf of country and your liberties. . . ."

Kate sat down again facing the window, Hagarty in her arms, purring contentedly. How wonderful it would be to be a cat now with no knowledge of the storm outside, of war, of death in automobiles. Where there was no knowledge at all of the future, and possibly little remembrance of the past. Where one's whole world was simply *now*. And *now*, for Hagarty, was a soft lap and a full stomach.

Kate determined that she would not get up again and look out until Roosevelt's speech was over, and she listened but hardly heard. Finally his talk came to an end: "Through that kind of peaceful service every nation can increase its happiness, banish the terrors of war, and abandon man's inhumanity to man.

"Never, in all our history, have Americans faced a job so well worthwhile. May it be said of us in the days to come that our children and our children's children rise up and call us blessed."

Kate put the cat down and, straining her eyes once again, gazed out the front window. All she could see was snow.

Nineteen

❄

"Hey, it's your kid's birthday," the boss told the mechanic at ten past eight that evening. "You can leave. Get home in time for the party and the president, too!"

Fred Espie put down his wrench and wiped his greasy hands on a rag from the back pocket of his overalls. He grinned at Zeke, who sat on a stool inside the filling station. "Let's go!" he said. "I got a party waiting!"

The mechanic drove a green 1934 DeSoto and kept it in fine shape, Zeke noticed. Mechanics could do that. If he had a car like that, he'd be halfway across the country by now. Head out to the desert maybe—live with the cotton-tails. Get some wild horses and start himself a little business. All he needed was a chance, but he didn't think he was about to find that here.

Hadn't anybody else ever made a mistake? Hadn't anyone in the jury ever run a red light? Hadn't the judge ever rolled past a stop sign? The difference, of course, was that his mistake had cost a life, and he was sure sorry about that. But the fact was that any of *their* mistakes could have cost a life too. They just hadn't, that's all. He wasn't one whit a better man for having been in prison than he was before. Just a little angrier, that's all.

"You got children?" Fred asked him as they made the turn onto Route 2. He flicked on his wipers to ward off the big white flakes that were floating down from the sky.

"No. Not married," Zeke replied.

"Well, Johnny's our first. Wife had a pretty hard time of it, so he's sort of special to us. Now he's a healthy twelve months, and whew! Got a pair of lungs you wouldn't believe."

Zeke smiled a little. They rode in silence for a few miles, the wipers lazily brushing the snow from the glass.

"Heard somebody say we've got high winds coming in tonight," the mechanic said. "Looks peaceful enough out there now—that southern breeze."

Zeke agreed. "Mild for March. Didn't realize so many folks came to town on Saturdays. Course, it's been a while . . ." He immediately wished he hadn't said that.

"Yeah? Where you been?"

"Oh, here and there. Looking for a job, actually, but not having much luck."

"Well, the way things are heating up in Europe, there'll be jobs go begging, now that they've started the draft. What do you think of the war?"

"Only one thing *to* think," Zeke replied. "We'll all be in it before too long, I'd imagine."

"Yeah. I got a deferment—back trouble—or I'd be drafted. Keep my mouth shut on the job, though. Don't want 'em to know just how much it hurts. What about you?"

"The same," said Zeke. "Trouble with my feet." It was all he could think of.

The mechanic glanced over at him again. "Well, we get into a shooting war, they'll be calling up married men, men with children, even us, I suppose. It sure don't look like a short-term thing to me. What'd you say your last name was, now?"

Zeke stiffened. He tried to remember if he'd given it before or not. Lied or not. The mechanic was new in the area, but he was living with in-laws near where Dwayne was living.

"Baxter," he said.

The mechanic rubbed one hand on his knee, as though trying to get the last of the grease off his fingers. The driver's seat, Zeke noticed, was already covered with old towels to protect the upholstery. "Seems I've heard that name before. Or was it Dexter?"

"I don't know," said Zeke. And then, "You can let me off at the turn, and you get on home to your little boy."

"You sure, now?"

Zeke was positive. He was farther away than he'd like to be, but if Fred Espie drove him all the way home, the mailbox right out there on the road said DEXTER on it, plain as day, and he'd know. If he'd heard anything at all, and he probably had, he'd remember that one of those Dexter boys went to prison. "A hop, a skip, and a jump, and I'm home," Zeke said. "Thanks for the lift. Enjoy the party." He had one hand on the door handle, the other on his satchel.

The mechanic slowed the car as he pulled over to the side, chuckling. "My wife's going to set the cake in front of him and let him dive in with both hands. Can't wait to see that." As Zeke got out Fred leaned forward and looked at the sky. "Now, that's what I call a nice snow."

"Thanks again," Zeke said, and closed the door. The mechanic gave a toot of the horn and went on, the beam from the DeSoto's headlights making a broad sweep over the fields as it pulled back onto the road again. The sound of the engine grew fainter and fainter as the taillights grew smaller in the distance and finally disappeared.

Zeke turned up the road toward Mekinock, the wind at his back, almost glad for the chance to walk. Couldn't be much more than a couple miles, and he'd walked it more times than he could count. It felt good to be hiking out here on the road all by himself, as a matter of fact—free to go any place he wanted. If he had the money, that is. He slipped one arm into a sleeve of his heavy jacket, then transferred the satchel to his left hand and slipped the other arm in. But he didn't fasten the zipper.

It was darker than he had anticipated, however. The moon, he had noticed the night before from the window of the bus, was almost full, and perhaps he'd been counting on that when he told the mechanic earlier he could find his way home. He figured he could make it to the house in forty minutes. He'd look a little frosty, maybe, and it would be a heck of a surprise when Dwayne opened the door and saw him there, though his brother wouldn't exactly celebrate, he imagined. Zeke would blame it on the telephone—the lack of one. "How you expect me to let you know I'm coming if you took out the darn phone?" he'd say.

He wasn't sure why it was he never got along with Dwayne. Got along with him as well as he got along with anyone, he imagined. Just two different personalities, was all. When you came right down to it, though, Zeke didn't especially want to share his life with anyone. Didn't like to feel obligated to anyone, judged by anyone, instructed by anyone. If life had anything to teach him, Zeke would discover it for himself. That's why he preferred horses to people, except he didn't have enough money to get out to where the horses were.

The sleeves of his heavy jacket were dusted now with snow, and flakes were beginning to cling to his eyelashes. If he could see where he was going better, he could walk a little faster, but the narrow country road was full of ruts and ridges that slowed him down.

He was walking north and was surprised suddenly to feel a blast of cold air meeting him head-on. As though someone had turned on a giant fan, the wind seemed to have switched from south to north, and with it, a drop in temperature.

"Hey, man!" he said aloud, and pulled up the zipper of his jacket.

Twenty

❄

Jesse and his dad were within sight of the house now. They had not quite reached the lane and could see the glow of the kerosene lamp back in the kitchen window. Jesse was talking about a basketball game of the previous night in Minnesota's District 31 championship tournament, giving his version of why Thief River Falls had won, when Doc Sterling suddenly said, "What on earth . . .?"

Jesse stopped gabbing and stared at the windshield. The snowflakes which had been big and beautiful not minutes before, had turned to a fine mist against the windshield, as though starting at the bottom and streaming upward. It looked to Jesse like a waterfall going the wrong way. At the same time there was a shrill whistle of wind coming in around the windows.

"What is it, Dad?" Jesse said as the car began to shake.

"I can't see a thing," the doctor said. It was as though

someone had thrown a sheet over the windshield, Jesse thought, and the wipers didn't help. His father braked to a stop.

"Dad, what *is* it?" Jesse asked again. It looked like they had run into a wall of snow.

"I sure don't know, but I'd say the snow has become a storm," Doc Sterling said, "and I'm not going anywhere until I can see the road." He turned off the engine.

"What if somebody comes along and runs into us?"

In answer, it felt as though the wind picked up the car and sent it a couple of feet backward.

"Man!" Jesse cried, his eyes wide.

"That wind's coming from the north, Jesse!" said his father. And repeated, "From the *North*!"

"You want me to get out and guide us home—walk alongside the car?" Jesse asked excitedly.

"You stay right here, Jesse. If we can't see one foot out the window, that means we can't see one foot in front of the car, either. We'll wait it out. Can't be more than a squall. Paper didn't say anything about a snowstorm, did it?"

"Not that I know," said Jesse.

The car shuddered and seemed to move sideways. Doc Sterling made sure it was in gear so they wouldn't be rolled, as he put it, "to kingdom come."

Even though all the windows were rolled up, Jesse could feel the wind coming in around them. "That air is really cold, Dad. Can you feel it?" he asked, putting his hand on the windshield.

"Well, I got a blanket back there if we need it. Got some tea and crackers, too, so we're not likely to starve or anything."

Jesse looked at him incredulously, trying to make out his face in the darkness. "You mean we could be here all night? With the house just up the road?"

"It could happen, but no one said anything about a storm, so I doubt it."

Jesse studied the strange look of the windshield.

"Have you ever been in a blizzard, Dad? I mean, caught out in one and couldn't get back?"

"My grandfather was. When I was growing up, all the old-timers talked about the big blizzard of 1888. He made it back okay but lost half his cattle." And then, sensing Jesse's silence perhaps, he added encouragingly, "No, I respect the weather. They tell me a blizzard's on the way, I pretty much stay put if I can. More than once I've been stranded in somebody's house overnight, but I've got enough sense not to go out when you can't see your hand in front of your face. That's why we're not getting out here."

Jesse figured it was something like waiting out a thunderstorm. Bad while it lasted—the lightning, thunder, and hail—but a storm that violent couldn't last forever.

But one hour later he and his dad were still sitting in the front seat of the Model A, while the wind howled worse than ever and shook the car.

Jesse noticed that his father had his arms folded across his chest, and every so often he rocked back and forth and stamped his feet. "Keep moving, Jesse," he said. "Keep that blood circulating." Then he began to recite poetry. First it was Robert Frost and his poem about stopping by the woods on a snowy evening. Then it was somebody Jesse didn't know. Most of Dad's poems, in fact, were by poets Jesse had never heard of:

"When icicles hang by the wall,
And Dick the shepherd blows his nail,
And Tom bears logs into the hall,
And milk comes frozen home in pail . . ."

Jesse listened in spite of himself, for this second poem ended with, "While greasy Joan doth keel the pot."

"What's 'blows his nail' and 'keel the pot'?" he asked.

His father laughed. "I don't know, but I always liked the sound of it. By guess who?"

"Who?"

"William Shakespeare."

"He should have put a little more work on it," Jesse offered, and his father laughed again. "Don't you know any poems about sun and summer and swimming and stuff? Something *warm*?"

"Oh, absolutely!" said Doc Sterling. "Let's see now, how does it go? 'When the . . . lark'? No. 'When the heat like a mist-veil floats, and poppies flame in the rye—'"

"I have to go to the bathroom, Dad," said Jesse.

The doctor turned and looked at him. "I used the bathroom at the Dryburgs', didn't you?"

"No. I don't like to use other people's bathrooms."

"We don't want to open the door and let in any more cold air than we have to, Jesse."

"Dad! I have to *go*!"

"There's an empty jug back there. Use that."

"No!" Jesse cried indignantly. "I'll just step outside of the car."

"You'll do no such thing. Either you hold it in or you use the jug."

For fifteen minutes more Jesse sat silent and sullen in the front seat. Finally he reluctantly crawled over into the back and rummaged about for the gallon jug.

"Don't look," he said.

"Don't worry," said Doc Sterling. "If you had two heads and purple hair, I still couldn't see you in the dark."

Twenty-One

✳

Kate stood at the window watching car lights coming down the road. The snow was heavy at times, but she could just make out the headlights and felt weak with relief when she recognized Gertie's half-closed lid. From a distance it appeared as one small headlight and one large one.

"They're here, Hagarty," she told the cat. "Well, not exactly here, but close." And she went to the kitchen to heat up the coffee for her father. When she returned to the parlor window to watch them pull in, she was startled to see only a dim blur of light where the car had been before, and then . . . nothing. It was as though a curtain of snow had dropped down over her window and she could barely see through it. She ran to a second window and saw the same.

Kate opened the front door and, as she stepped out, shrieked when a rush of wind swept her off the front stoop and into a snowbank. Too astonished to cry out, she crawled back up on her hands and knees, gasping and clutching at the stoop, then hurled herself inside the open doorway, where Hagarty stood seemingly frozen to the floor, his fur standing on end. Finally she made it to her feet and, using both hands, managed to shove the door closed against the howling wind.

She stomped the snow off her shoes, shook out her clothes and hair, and was surprised to find there was grit in her mouth along with the snow. The wind was like a tornado! And where could all that snow have come from? It could hardly be that deep so soon, unless the wind had driven it into a drift.

"My gosh!" she said aloud. "It knocked me right off my feet!"

She went to the window again, her eyes in the direction she had faced before. But this time she saw nothing at all. No car, no lights, no trees or fence or barn or moon—just a blanket of white, as though she had suddenly gone blind.

At almost the same time, weather warnings were coming over the radio, half drowned out now by static. All she heard were words like "wind" and "snow" and "falling temperatures" and "livestock." She did hear the warnings, "Remain in your home. Remain in your car . . ."

They've gone off the road! she thought. She could almost see in her mind the very place they had stopped beside the pasture.

"I can't believe this!" she said to Hagarty. "One minute I could see their car coming, and the next minute I couldn't see a thing."

Still, she almost expected to hear them drive in, regardless. They must be within fifty feet of the driveway. The road was so straight and her father knew it so well, he could probably reach home by dead reckoning. Failing that, they could probably get out and find the house on foot.

Instantly her father's warnings came to mind: *Never* try to walk in a snowstorm unless you are already outside and need to find shelter. You could not grow up in North Dakota without hearing the tales of farmers who had gone out to the barn to milk their cows and got lost on their way back to the house. The wife who went out to see about the turkeys and was found frozen to death three feet from the shed. Farmers strung lines between their house and barn to guide them through a blizzard, and there was still a wire, strung by the previous owner, running from the Sterlings' house to the barn.

The rawness of needing her mother suddenly stung like a cut on the skin. Mother would have known what to do. How comforting it would be simply to turn to her now and say, "What should we do?" and let her make the decisions. And once again it came unbidden, her hatred of Zeke Dexter, like a haunting. If she were to see *him* on the road right now . . .

No, she told herself. She had other things to think about at the moment. She would call their nearest neighbors, the Finleys, and see what they might suggest. She lifted the receiver from the hook and rang the operator, but no one answered. No doubt telephone lines were jammed.

Kate waited five minutes and tried again, but this time when she put the receiver to her ear, she could tell that the phone was dead. Perhaps the lines were down. She realized then that the party line had not rung at all since her last call to the Dryburgs.

She stared at the receiver before placing it slowly back on the hook. Then she walked to the kitchen window and held the kerosene lamp close to the glass to see the thermometer. She could just make out the large black numbers. In an hour it had dropped from twenty-eight degrees to thirteen. The outside door to the back porch rattled in the wind, and the shutters banged and clanked against the house even though they were fastened securely.

Kate remembered what Mother had done a few times when her father was out in a storm. In a cupboard by the back door were the rest of the kerosene lamps. Kate lit three and carried one to the front window in the parlor, and two upstairs to place in windows there. You never knew how far someone caught in a storm might wander, or in which direction he was likely to turn. Sometimes a lantern in the window was the only thing that stood between a traveler freezing to death and a traveler being saved.

Now, what else could she do? She went back down to the kitchen and stood motionless in the center of the floor. She could almost hear her own heart beat.

The radio, that was it. She *must* keep the radio going, her only link to the outside. Taking a kerosene lamp, she went to the cellar to crank the generator herself and restore the batteries.

The cellar seemed darker than it had ever looked before, and a cobweb brushing across her face made her jump. Holding the lamp in front of her, she made her way over to the generator. She set the lamp down and grasped the handle of the Delco. Then, just as she had seen her father do, she gave it two cranks. Nothing happened.

At the same time, she thought she heard a noise upstairs,

footsteps, possibly. Her heart raced and she felt perspiration trickle down her sides beneath her arms. Convinced finally that the sounds were mere creakings of an old house, she grasped the handle once again with both hands, and this time gave it one . . . two . . . three . . . hard, quick cranks, and it caught.

Kate let out her breath and shivered from the feel of her own sweat. But the hum of the generator was comforting— a familiar sound—and the fact that she had succeeded at something gave her confidence.

When she went upstairs, she took the lamp with her and checked every room, every closet, half expecting to find someone in it. But there were no tracks on the floor, no sign of entry, and both doors remained locked.

Once again Kate went to the front window, and once again she saw nothing.

She took the coffee off the stove.

Twenty-Two

It was the darndest thing Zeke had ever experienced. He'd worked on construction crews from time to time, so he was used to the heat of the plains in summer and the dead cold of a Dakota winter. But he had never gone through as sudden a change as this one. It was as though he had walked into a meat locker, it was that swift and that chilling.

The snow fell faster and heavier, then heavier still. And all at once it was like a gigantic snowplow coming right at him, pushing a wall of snow and ice, for as it hit his face it seemed more than snow—slivers of ice perhaps, filling his nose and sealing his eyes shut. Coughing, he spat and found his mouth full of dust and grit.

He held his satchel in front of his face for protection, then turned his back to the wind, struggling to stay upright. Still the wind howled around him. He raised his jacket collar so it extended under the flaps of his cap, and began walking backward in the gale, stumbling to his knees a time or two from the force of the wind.

It was cold and getting colder. Each time the storm slackened momentarily, when the wind took a breather, Zeke faced forward again and tried to walk faster. But even then it seemed he took three steps forward to the two he was blown back. Once he found himself tumbling, rolling, ending up with his feet in a snowbank. He struggled to get up and stomped the snow off his boots to keep his feet as dry as possible. It wouldn't do to get wet.

He should be up to the house shortly. If Dwayne had a light on, Zeke could probably see it from here. Even as he thought it, however, he realized he would not be able to see it at all, for he could see nothing, not even when he held his hand in front of his nose.

"Son of a gun," he said in astonishment.

Then he realized he was not walking on the road at all. He could feel that the ground beneath him was a field—the *crack* and *crunch* of frozen grass, the pits and potholes in the soil. He turned slowly around, the wind slapping his face like an angry father. Which way had he been headed? In what direction was home? Had the wind been coming at him from the north or the northwest?

He tried to gauge his direction from the wind, but at times it seemed to come from all sides at once. Zeke was not one to worry, however. When you'd spent three and a half years in prison, nobody caring to give you the time of day and some of the prisoners looking for every little way to torment you, you'd already seen one of the worst things that could happen to you. You didn't get too alarmed over a sudden snowstorm that would probably blow itself out in twenty or thirty minutes. On a springlike day in March the snow didn't last all that long, and this one had sneaked in so quietly not even the weather fellows seemed to know it was coming.

At the same time, Zeke wished he had a second pair of gloves under his heavy leather pair. Tucking the satchel under one arm, he thrust his hands in the pockets of his jacket, and that helped. He remembered the double gloves he had worn one winter laying pipe. Even then he'd felt he could use a third pair.

His first faint stirrings of alarm came when he realized he had probably been walking most of an hour and had not stumbled across anything leading to a house. Not a mailbox or telephone pole, not a fence or shed. He tried to remember what *was* around his and Dwayne's house that he could put a hand on. A mailbox by the road, the stump of an oak tree on the other side of their driveway. But he was not on a road, of that he was certain, so there would be no mailbox to guide him in.

He felt the weariness first in his legs. He wasn't used to walking like this and had lost a lot of strength in his lower body in prison. A walk around the prison yard in the morning, another in the evening maybe; the sit-ups he did in his cell. The captain had put him on kitchen duty the last couple of years, and there he carried in heavy milk cans of a morning, unloaded sacks of potatoes, carried the bushels of apples to storage, so that his arms were in reasonably good shape, but not his legs. And his feet seemed to have flattened some—wider maybe—because his boots felt a little tight. Or were they shrinking in the snow he found himself in now?

It did not seem possible, but the air was growing even colder. It must be in the teens by now. He knew what zero felt like, and it wasn't there yet, but the temperature was sliding downward. He made up his mind that the first house he came to, he would knock. One thing about Dakotans, they always took you in. Especially during a snowstorm. And if he couldn't find a house, he'd take whatever shelter he could find—a barn, a shed, a chicken house even.

The storm did not ease up. The wind, in fact, increased, and the snow continued to fall. Zeke discovered with horror that he was growing sleepy, and his face was freezing.

"Now, see here," he told himself. "Walk! Talk! Keep your eyes open. You stop, you're dead." And he discovered something else about himself: that although he had thought from time to time in prison that it would make no difference to anyone if he were alive or dead, he did not want to die. He might be worthless, of no use to a living soul, but he still craved the chance to start over.

Zeke stopped and opened his satchel. He took out the white shirt he had worn before the judge and wrapped it twice around his face, all but his eyes, tying the sleeves behind him. Then he took out his good trousers and wound them around his neck like a scarf.

He put his mind on the desert—on horses—of riding bareback, perhaps, across a hot, burning desert, the heat of the horse under his thighs, the sweat of the animal soaking the calves of his pant legs, the snort of the beast, the blistery sun on his neck and shoulders, the perspiration-soaked hat on his head, the feel of the leather reins in his hand.

"Move!" he ordered his feet. And he moved. He figured he had been walking about two hours now. Or was it three? Or only one? He could not see his watch.

He decided at last to change direction. Clearly he was finding nothing here and could not fathom where he might be, except in the vast, untended fields between the road to his house and the next road over. There was no point in going back in the direction he had come, even if he could retrace his steps for certain, because there had been nothing behind him either.

Go right or left, then, he told himself, and he chose the direction the wind was less severe. Again Zeke set out, trying to make time when there was a lull in the wind, bracing himself when it roared up again. The constant movement of his feet, he figured, was all that kept them from freezing. He wiggled his toes inside his boots, wiggled his fingers inside his gloves.

He stumbled once over a low, unkempt barbed-wire fence and thought of following it along until it took him somewhere. But it ended in a snowbank, and he hadn't the strength to dig through it. When he tried to find it again on the other side, it was lost. So was he.

At one point he put his hand to the shirt around his face and was startled to discover it was frosted over with a paper-thin sheet of ice. His eyebrows had frozen hard. He swore and hit at his eyebrows with one gloved hand.

Too exhausted to go farther, he simply stayed put the next time the wind knocked him down, and for a moment he lay with his cheek resting on one sleeve. How easy it would be to sleep and just let go. Pass on. Let the snow cover him, an easy burial. Dwayne wouldn't have to bother.

"No!" he said suddenly, still connected to life. He swore again, at himself this time, and ordered himself up on his hands and knees and began to crawl, leaving his satchel behind. Once again his frozen body moved, his clothes creaking and crackling as he plodded along on his knees. Then he got to his feet and stumbled blindly on, waving his arms like a madman in order to keep his circulation going, beating them against his chest, stamping his feet. *Live, live, live!*

Twenty-Three

❄

"I'm cold, Dad!"

Jesse couldn't seem to stop shivering. He had eaten two crackers but didn't want any tea for fear he would need a bathroom again. The thought of using the jug was too gross for words.

"Jesse, I want you to do five more climbs into the rear seat and back. Make it six."

"Dad!"

"Do as I say!" There was both impatience and uneasiness in his father's voice.

Jesse got up on his knees on the passenger side, turning around, and awkwardly hoisted himself over the back, tumbling into the pile of his dad's "necessaries" on the floor. Then he turned and went headfirst over into the front seat again, his legs flying every which way, one foot landing on his dad's shoulder. He did it again and again, but after the fourth climb he stayed where he was in the front seat and pulled the car blanket up around his chin.

"Your turn," he said from under the blanket.

This took some doing and always got them laughing.

And laughter was becoming more scarce after three hours in a freezing car.

Doc Sterling, big as a bear, proceeded to maneuver himself out from under the steering wheel, then turning around, hauled himself up over the back of the front seat.

"Ow!" Jesse giggled. "Your knee's on my leg, Dad!"

"So take off your leg," the doctor said, and they laughed again.

Puffing and grunting, the top of the seat digging into his belly, Doc Sterling reached for the backseat with his hands, then picked up his feet to the edge of the front seat and started over.

"And . . . he's *off*!" Jesse said irrepressibly, giving him a push from behind, and the doctor sprawled onto the backseat with a squealing of springs.

While he was back there, he dug around in his supplies for the extra sweater and instructed Jesse to wrap it around his thighs—wherever he felt coldest. The raincoat came next. Then he gathered himself together, disentangled himself from the backseat clutter, and edged over into the front of the car again. All the while the howl of the wind accompanied his huffs and puffs, and snow was accumulating inside along the windows, driven around the glass by the ferocity of the gale.

"Dad, if only we had a heater . . ."

"I know, Jesse."

"Wouldn't it be better to leave the car and try to make it to the house? I'll bet we could find it."

"Don't even think that. Don't *ever* try that, ever!"

They huddled together, sharing the warmth of their bodies, and the doctor vigorously rubbed his son's arms and legs. "Keep moving your feet," he said. "Stamp those feet, Jesse!"

"I can't hardly feel them anymore," Jesse said. "They're like big clumps of ice."

"Move them anyway." Doc Sterling hurled himself into the backseat again, and Jesse heard him ripping apart the sacks and a cardboard box he had there. He dumped them in the front seat before he returned, and set about fashioning insulation around Jesse's legs and feet.

Jesse felt his eyes beginning to close, and his head gave a quick jerk.

"Jesse!" said his dad. "Give me the multiplication tables."

"What?"

"Recite the multiplication tables for me."

"Dad, I *know* my multiplication. We learned that in third grade!"

"Recite them anyway. Go ahead. I've got to know if you're falling asleep, and I can't see your face in the dark."

Jesse recited all that he could, but when he felt himself drifting off to sleep again, he heard his father say, "Batters and batting averages. Give me everyone you can think of, Jesse. Let's start with Ty Cobb. . . ."

"Lifetime?"

"Yep."

"It was .367."

"What about Walter Johnson?"

This was better than multiplication, but all the while Jesse's lips were moving, his eyes wanted to close. His head wanted to sleep. He knew the danger, however, and had moved on to runs scored when there came another shudder and rocking in the wind, and the car turned a bit more.

Jesse looked over at his dad. The white snow covering the windows made the interior of the car light enough to distinguish each other faintly. "Which way do you suppose we're facing now, Dad?"

"I don't know. We might be turned completely around." Doc Sterling punched him playfully on his arm. "C'mon. Wrestle with me."

"What?"

"We've got to keep moving, Jesse. It's the only way to stay warm."

"I'm really tired."

"No, you're not! Wrestle!"

It was an order, not a suggestion. They grappled and twisted and turned. And when they were out of breath, they rested a moment, then went at it again, this time so hard that the car seemed to be knocking.

"Dad!" Jesse yelled suddenly. "Somebody's out there!"

His father sat up, listening. The sound came again. It was not the wind. Someone was knocking.

"Yes! Yes! We're here!" he yelled. "Jesse, it's on your side. Open the door."

Jesse twisted around in the seat.

"Maybe Kate saw us coming and guessed what happened," the doctor said. "Maybe she called the highway crew and they've come."

"I can't get it open, Dad! It's frozen!" Jesse said, panting.

Doc Sterling leaned across Jesse's legs and pushed with both hands against the door as Jesse kicked at it with his feet.

The car door opened slowly, for something seemed to be propped against it, but then a gloved hand reached inside, a jacket sleeve, and what appeared to be an apparition to Jesse—a man, eyes hidden beneath thick, icy brows, a shirt wrapped around his face like a mask, his head encased in ice, bent jerkily down to get in the car. Suddenly he fell forward across Jesse's lap and lay still.

Twenty-Four

Zeke felt as though his body would crack in two. As he fell forward into the car the creaking of his frozen clothes sounded like the snapping of bones. And though he could feel nothing, he imagined his spine giving way.

He didn't know or care how many people were in the car, but he heard voices:

"Jesse, here! Help me pull him in."

"Is he dead, Dad?"

"Get his feet. I don't think he can lift them. Then crawl in the backseat."

Hands were grappling at him, pulling, tugging. His knees did not seem to bend and he was dragged across the front seat right onto the chest of a large man behind the steering wheel.

Somebody was crawling over his legs. There was a slam of the car door. Then the weight was off his legs and a boy's voice from the backseat repeated itself: "Is he dead?"

"I don't think so. Half dead maybe."

Zeke felt fingers encircling his wrist, pressing down.

"He's got a pulse, but not a very strong one. You, sir." Zeke felt hands gripping his coat and shaking him. "Can you tell me your name?" More shaking. "What's your name, sir?"

All he wanted was to sleep.

"Jesse, under that box of Gertie's spare parts back there you'll find a couple old newspapers. I want you to start crumpling the pages up and hand them to me. I'm going to stuff this man's clothes full of insulation. His coat's wet, but I hate to take it off unless we have to."

Gertie. Jesse. The names swam in Zeke's head, but he didn't try to connect them. He was so glad to have a place to lie down, his head against the man's chest. Just let him sleep.

Then he was being pushed upright again, made to sit up, and the moment he was upright, he slumped to the other side, his head against the side window.

The man behind the steering wheel was trying to unzip his jacket, was flicking the ice off his chest. For a moment Zeke tried to open his eyes, but there was still ice on the lashes, and when they opened at last, he felt as though he were looking out of a cave with icicles hanging at the entrance. He could just make out the dashboard of a car, indistinct in the darkness.

But the voice was addressing him again. "What's your name, fella? Where you from? Come on, talk to me."

Zeke could only think of where he had been, but his lips wouldn't move. Even his tongue was stiff. He tried to say "Bismarck," but the man didn't understand.

"Mark?" the man asked.

Zeke tried again. "Bi . . . mar . . ."

"Bill Mark? That it? Well, Bill, you've had a close call, but we're going to do what we can here. Jesse, can you find that jar of tea?"

The rim of a Mason jar was pressed against Zeke's lips. He managed to get a mouthful, but the next one ran down the front of his jacket.

"There's more if you want it," the man said. Then, "Jesse, can you give me a hand here? I've got his jacket unzipped. See if you can stuff some of those newspapers down the back of his neck, and I'll try to stuff the front of him and his sleeves. Try to get them right next to his skin, because his clothes are wet. You stay awake, now, fella. Keep talking to us. I'm George Sterling and this is Jesse. You live around here?"

Zeke's eyes found the dark of the ceiling and stayed there, open wide. *Sterling?* This wasn't making any sense. What was he doing at the doctor's place? What was the doctor doing out here in his car? He had walked out of prison and right into the hands of the folks who hated him most. Had a right to hate him. He lapsed into a dream. They were stuffing his clothes with newspapers the way you'd start a fire.

"Hey!" he said suddenly, his body bolting forward.

"Easy, now, easy!" Doc Sterling said.

"We're just trying to get you warm, mister," said the boy.

Jesse must be his kid.

"You want another drink of tea?" asked the doctor. And Zeke heard him say to Jesse, "Don't know how long he's been out there, but several hours, I'm guessing, from the look of things."

Zeke felt himself slowly coming out of his fog and began shivering violently. He was starting to feel pain in his toes, his fingers. A chunk of ice fell off his eyebrows. He moved his tongue around in his mouth and took another swallow of cold tea.

"Jesse," the doctor was saying. "Look around in that box of spare parts and see if you can find a working flashlight. There's at least two of them, but I don't know that the batteries are any good." And then to Zeke, "How long have you been out in this storm, Bill? It's past midnight."

"Uuuh . . . long . . . time," Zeke replied, trying to get his tongue, his lips, to work. What would they say when they knew? Should he get out? Couldn't. Couldn't walk anymore.

"Car stalled somewhere?" the doctor asked.

"No . . . car . . ."

"Where do you live?"

"O . . . er . . . uh . . . brother . . ."

"Live with your brother? Where's that? He's not out in this blizzard too, is he?"

"Don't . . . know."

"He's still got ice on his ears, Jesse," Doc Sterling was saying. "Any luck with those flashlights?"

"This is the only one that's working, Dad," said the boy, and something fell over the front seat against Zeke's thigh. The doctor picked it up and a faint circle of light fell on the dashboard. Then the doctor checked Zeke's frost-nipped ears, his nose, his chin. He beamed the flashlight directly into Zeke's eyes and opened both lids of each eye in turn with his fingers.

And suddenly the doctor reared backward, as Zeke knew was bound to happen.

"What's the matter, Dad?" asked Jesse. And when his father didn't answer, he asked, "What *is* it?"

"It's Zeke," the doctor said.

Twenty-Five

Kate was tormented by indecision. She knew from the newscasts that this was a blizzard that had caught the plains states by surprise. Already deaths were being reported. Travelers were trapped in cars. Students were stranded in gymnasiums after games. Audiences were not allowed to leave theaters. Her father and brother were trapped in their car not a hundred yards from the house. The phone was dead and there was no one she could call on to help.

She sat down facing the window, hands in her lap, almost paralyzed with fear. There was time to think, however, she told herself, and she tried to conjure up what her mother would do if she were here. Mother always kept her calm; she would know. If only Kate had told her *that* the evening Mother left for choir practice and never came back. That Kate could count on her. Appreciated her. *Loved* her.

She shook her head violently to get it back on track. *Think,* she instructed herself. First, her father had been in storms before and he did have at least a blanket with him, she knew that much. And tea and crackers.What else, she wasn't sure.

Second, he knew enough not to try to get out and walk somewhere in a blizzard. She could count on him not to do that. He surely knew he was close to home, and when the weather let up, he and Jesse would walk in.

That should have reassured her, but it didn't. There were all those what-ifs. What if her father had had a heart attack and that's why the car stopped? What if Jesse had tried to strike out on his own to get help and was lost in the storm? What if Jesse was sick and his father decided to try to find the house anyway? What if they stayed in the car but the blizzard went on for two or three days and buried the car completely?

Go, Kate! . . .Stay, Kate! . . .Go, stay, stay, go. . . . She sucked in her breath shakily and covered her ears. Around her, the bones and joints of the old house creaked and groaned, buffeted by the wind.

By one in the morning she had a plan. She would go, and that decision made, she felt better. She would not take a single step where she could not hold on to something familiar. The wire stretched from house to barn would get her that far. It was what she would do after she reached the barn that troubled her—after she went out the doors leading to the pasture.

She decided that she would follow the fence from the barn all the way down to the road and see if she could reach the car from there. Second thought: There was a large section of fence down as you neared the road. She would have nothing to hold on to. She could not try that.

Plan B: She would have to go the long way around, then. When she went out the back doors of the barn, she would have to follow the fence the other way, around the whole perimeter of the pasture, and get to the road from that direction. It would take longer, of course, but what could be dangerous about that as long as she was always, always holding on to the fence? She would follow it until she reached the road and then . . .

Then what would she do? Where the fence ran along the road, she would have to climb over it in order to find the car. What if she couldn't see it from the fence? What if she had to let go and search blindly with her hands? There was also a ditch to cross.

She went to the cellar for the package of new clothesline rope, unopened. Only fifty feet, but perhaps that's all she would need to tether herself to the fence and explore along the ditch and the road. She also found a seventy-five-foot package of drapery cord. She would take that, too. Kate felt excited. Energized.

"Hagarty," she said. "You'll have to stay in the cellar till I get back." She did not want a cat jumping up on a windowsill, upsetting a kerosene lamp. Hagarty opened his eyes when she picked him up, and shook himself when she set him on the top of the cellar stairs. But because he liked to explore and was rewarded with an occasional mouse, he did not complain when she closed the door behind him.

Kate dressed with care, from her toes up. Three pairs of light socks, topped by heavy wool kneesocks, to be worn with heavy shoes and lined boots. Flannel pajama bottoms, covered by wool slacks, then snow pants. Long-sleeved underwear over her bra and vest, and a wool shirt on top of that. A wool sweater, toboggan cap, and hooded winter jacket. Her red flannel scarf to tie around her nose and mouth. Gloves and mittens both. She read the temperature again through the kitchen window. Two below zero. She thought again of what Jesse and her dad were wearing. Now she was more determined than ever to go.

Kate checked the kerosene lamps at the windows to be sure they were anchored securely and were at the best possible vantage point for a traveler to see. She left both front and back doors unlocked so that people could find their way in, if necessary. Then, thrusting the package of clothesline rope in one pocket, the cord in the other, she took a flashlight, crossed the back porch, and opened the outer door to a rush of wind and snow. Feeling for the wire line attached to the house, she grasped it securely and stepped off the porch.

It was impossible to tell if it was still snowing or if the wind was whipping snow around her in its fury. The wind did not seem quite as strong as it had before when it knocked her off the front stoop, but it was strong enough that she had to fight it with each step to stay upright.

She could see nothing—no sky, no moon, no barn, no trees—a swirl of white fog in the darkness, snow stinging her eyelids, and the *cold*. What little forehead that was exposed ached with the cold's intensity.

How could anyone survive who was caught out in this? she wondered as she lifted each foot out of knee-deep snow. She ran her hand along the wire, knowing she could not let go for a moment. Once, she fell down and was terrified that she would not be able to grasp it again. For ten seconds or so her arms flailed about in desperation, before her wrist struck it and she held on tight.

At the barn, however, she found she could not open the doors without digging the snow away that had piled up against them. Getting down on her hands and knees, she dug and scraped and pushed until she could wedge one of the doors open just enough to squeeze inside.

The only thing better about the barn was that it sheltered her from the wind. It seemed almost as cold. She was used to North Dakota winters, having lived near Grand Forks all her life, but she did not like them and went outside in winter as little as possible. She took after her mother that way. It occurred to her that she should have left a note on the kitchen table about what she was going to do and the time she had left the house. What if Dad or Jesse stumbled in to find her gone? Would they go out in the blizzard to look for her?

She would not go back. To go back meant the possibility existed that she would get lost in the snow, and she simply would not allow that to happen. She took a moment to stomp the snow off her boots and snow pants, then went to the doors at the other end of the barn.

They would not open at all. Kate realized that this side of the barn, facing west, had received far more than its share of snow, and it was here on the northwest side that the drifts would be deepest. Not only here but all along the fence. Even if she were to get the door open by some miracle, there would be snow drifts by the side of the barn and along the entire length of the fence. All this time and all this effort for nothing, and she had no idea what was happening to Jesse and her dad in the car.

Twenty-Six

Jesse sat stunned in the backseat, staring at the shadowy head of the man who was sitting in their car now, in Jesse's seat, in this blizzard, drinking their tea. Zeke was supposed to be in prison for another year and a half!

"What'd he do, Dad? Escape?" he asked.

Doc Sterling himself, turned sideways on the seat, his back to the steering wheel, didn't seem to know what to make of it either. He kept the flashlight focused on Zeke.

"How'd you get here, Zeke?" he asked.

"Bus," Zeke answered numbly, as though his tongue were anesthetized. "From Bis . . . mar. . . . They le' me go. Early release . . ."

Jesse waited for an explanation from his father, and his dad said, "You can get early release for good behavior, Jesse."

"Good behavior?" Jesse said incredulously.

Another spasm of shivering overtook Zeke, and he

hugged himself with his arms, the crumpled paper inside his jacket rustling loudly.

"You took a bus from Bismarck to Grand Forks, then?" Doc Sterling asked.

"Yeah."

"And you were on your way out here to see me, or what?"

"N—no." Zeke's teeth were chattering now. "Going home."

"Your place, you mean?" the doctor asked.

"Yeah. Me and Dwayne's."

Jesse's mouth fell open. "Why, that burned down!" he said.

He saw Zeke's head turn toward his father.

"That's right, Zeke. Just a few days ago. Nobody told you? Think that old stove in the kitchen had developed a crack—what the firemen said, anyway. Dwayne wasn't home, but everything's gone, I'm afraid." Jesse wondered how his dad could sound so polite to this man. Cold, but polite.

A prolonged exclamation came from Zeke's chest, and he hunched over as though he'd been punched in the stomach. Finally he straightened and asked, "Where's Dwayne now? You know?"

"Someone said he's rooming with another man from the power company till he can find a place. You'll have to ask around."

Jesse saw the man's head tip back. He himself sat without moving. It was the first time he'd been near a convict. He waited for his dad to say something, but it was Zeke who spoke next.

"About . . . what happened to your wife . . . ," he said.

"You know I never meant that to be . . . what I did," he said. "I never meant to hurt anyone."

But you did! Jesse thought. He said nothing, however, waiting for a cue from his father. Would his dad turn Zeke out of the car?

"I know," Doc Sterling replied finally. Then, business-like, he focused the flashlight on Zeke's nose and said to Jesse, "This man has a frostbitten nose. You take the flashlight and look in my bag back there, find me some of those heavy gauze pads he can hold against his face. Probably got more than his nose frostbitten, but I'm not about to take his shoes off till we can get to some place warm."

For a moment Jesse didn't move. Who cared about Zeke Dexter's nose? He himself was freezing, his dad was freezing, but Doc Sterling left no room for debate. Jesse took the flashlight, opened his father's worn black bag, and began searching through it for the gauze.

Twenty-Seven

❄

Kate was in a frenzy now. The more she was blocked in her effort to reach her father and Jesse, the more determined she became. Stubborn, Jesse called her. Maybe she was.

There was nothing in that one hundred yards of pasture between the barn and the road except the old windmill, about forty yards down. Even with the clothesline rope and the cord tied together, it would never reach from barn to road, but perhaps if she could find the windmill . . .

Turning on the flashlight and propping it up on the rusty plow left by the previous owner, Kate took off her gloves and mittens, opened the packages of rope and cord. Carefully she tied them end to end, testing her square knot to be sure it would hold. She put on her gloves and mittens again and looped the rope around her arm like a lasso.

She was cold. In the light from the flashlight Kate ran around inside the barn until she began to feel she might perspire. She did not want to sweat. She wanted to work out each detail of her plan before she left.

If she tied the rope to something in the barn, and the other end around her waist, she could try to reach the windmill. If she did, she would untie the rope from her waist, pull it taut, and tie it to the windmill. Then, holding onto the rope like a hand rail, she would follow it back to the barn, untie the end of the rope there, tie *that* end around her waist, and follow it back to the windmill again. The problem she was wrestling with now was how she could mark her path from barn to windmill so that once the rope was untied in the barn, she could still find her way back.

On the last lap of the barn's perimeter, she stumbled upon one of the green pickets that used to surround Mother's vegetable garden, and saw the rest lying loose and scattered in one corner.

Why not use the pickets? Pickets stuck in the snow. She went over her plan again to make sure she had thought of everything. Then she opened one of the barn windows nearest the road and laboriously dumped an armful of pickets out onto the ground. Another armful and another, the wind grasping at her like some old witch each time she leaned out.

Tying one end of her rope to the seat of the rusty plow, she tied the other around her waist and hoisted herself up over the sill; she half jumped, half fell into the snow outside.

She picked up as many pickets as she could carry and stood for a moment with her back against the barn, trying to get her bearings in the fog of swirling snow. She could only guess the right direction, for the flashlight beam could not penetrate the snow ahead. She might well be wrong, but she started out on what she hoped was the way to the windmill.

To Kate, it seemed that the wind was on fiercely intimate terms with her, licking at her eyelids with an insistent tongue, probing under the edge of the red flannel scarf as though trying to uncover her neck, forcing itself up the sleeves of her heavy jacket, despite the sweater she wore beneath. Kate kept going.

She felt the snow deepening suddenly as she sank in up to her knees, then her thighs. She was either closer to the ditch out by the road than she had imagined, or the snow was piled up against something, the drift getting deeper and deeper. And then, to her utter amazement, she bumped something with her knee, followed by her shoulder. She put out one hand, and even through the layers of leather and wool she could feel the cold metal supports of the windmill. Pure, blind luck.

As much as she had wanted to find it, however, now she wondered if she should go on. She estimated she had left the house forty or fifty minutes ago, and even under all her clothing, prepared as she was for subzero weather, she had never felt this cold.

Every movement she made was awkward, every step she took cumbersome. What would have been a simple task in normal temperatures in daylight hours—untying the end of the rope from around her waist, pulling it taut so she could follow it back to the barn, and fastening it to the windmill—became a project that tried her patience. First she had to drop the pickets she'd been carrying. Then she took the flashlight from her coat pocket, removed the scarf from around her face, turned on the flashlight, and held it in her mouth; she took off her mittens, pulling the rope as tight as she could, and then tied it to the windmill. When she had succeeded at last, she put her mittens back on, thrust the flashlight in her pocket, picked up the pickets, and made her way back along the taut rope, placing pickets in the snow beneath the line, anchoring them securely so she could find them again.

When she reached the barn, she climbed back in, untied the rope from the plow, tied it around her waist and climbed back out. She had toyed with the idea of running around inside the barn again to warm herself, but she was too worried now about Jesse and her dad. If she was this cold, having been out only an hour or so, what was happening to them?

Scooping up from the snow outside the window all of the remaining pickets she could carry, she followed the ones she had already stuck in the snow, the rope going slack. Fear reared up inside her again. What if the wind blew them over? What if she got out as far as the windmill and couldn't find her way back?

The snow should have brightened the landscape. She could remember nights when, standing outside after a new snow, the round moon a large white eye in the sky, she had felt she could see everything as clear as day. But now the blowing snow made a whiteout; only now and then, when the wind died for a moment, did she think she saw the tall gray outline of the windmill. But it disappeared again in the next gust.

There was only one other landmark that might guide her—the pine tree at the end of the driveway—but she could not see that at all. When at last she reached the windmill, she dropped her second load of pickets, catching her thumb on the round metal eye at the top of one, the picket Mother had used to latch a makeshift gate to the fence around her garden. Then, feeling her way along with her hands and feet, she moved around the base of the windmill until she came to the pump that brought up water for the horse trough.

She stood very still. If the pump was here and the windmill there, that meant she was facing south, and the road was east of the barn. She turned toward the east then and, walking sideways to keep the direction straight in her mind, she blindly retraced her steps back to the pile of pickets, gathered them up in her arms, and set out for what she hoped would be the road and the place she imagined the car to be.

With every other step she pushed a picket into the snow, her burden growing lighter as she went. Yet she was not at all sure that she was heading the right way, and she had to stop every so often and disentangle the dangling rope from a picket. If she did not reach the road, she might have to backtrack and remove all the stakes, starting out in another direction.

She turned on her flashlight, but again the blowing snow was impenetrable. Her father's car could be right in front of her nose and she could walk right past it.

To her dismay, she soon ran out of pickets. She'd lost some in the snow, she knew. There were still a few yards of rope left, she guessed, and she moved gingerly around, trying to reach the fence by the ditch, hoping her calculations were off and it might be closer than she expected. That if she got this far, she might somehow be able to see the car. But the rope became taut, and she could go no farther. The road, she guessed, was still fifty feet away.

In frustration and disappointment, she felt tears welling up and immediately checked herself. They could only freeze her eyelids shut. She could not afford the luxury of crying.

She shouted instead.

"Dad!" she screamed, turning in one direction, then another, her eyes scanning the place she thought the road might be. "Jesse! . . . Dad! . . . Jesse! . . ." Over and over.

And then to her left, perhaps twenty yards from where she stood, she saw a faint gleam of yellow light flash on and off from behind the snow.

Twenty-Eight

❋

There were tingling sensations in his fingers and toes now, so Zeke knew that at least they hadn't frozen solid. At the doctor's urging, he had forced himself to crawl over the front seat and into the back just to keep his body in motion, but it was so awkward and exhausting, he would not try again. He was too tired to move, too cold to care, and there was no place to go home to if he survived. His only use at this point was to provide one more body in the car to heat it up for Jesse and his father. This was what he had become.

Jesse, in turn, had crawled up front and was curled on the passenger seat now, wrapped in the car blanket. Doc Sterling was trying to get the kid to wrestle with him.

"I'm tired, Dad," the boy kept saying, and his teeth chattered with the cold. "Leave me alone."

"Jesse, you have to move around. You can't go to sleep. It's important!" his father said.

"When it gets light, Dad, then I'll go out and we can walk home."

"That's several hours off, Jesse, and I don't know if we're under five inches or five feet of snow. If the blizzard keeps up, it could snow for three days. You have to stay awake, now," the doctor said, but Zeke noticed that even his voice was sounding tired, strained. And when he got no reply, Doc Sterling half turned in his seat and said, "Hand me that coffee tin on the floor back there, Zeke. I'm going to build a fire."

Zeke wasn't sure he'd heard right. "Inside the car?" he asked.

"Right up here on the floor," the doctor said.

Zeke leaned down till his arm could drag the floor—through sacks and boxes of this and that, till his numbed fingers curled around the smooth round rim of a coffee tin.

"You're going to build a fire in *that*?" Jesse asked as Doc Sterling gave him the flashlight to hold and set the can on the floor.

"Why, this coffee tin has more uses than you can shake a stick at," Jesse's father said. "It's been my sink, my toilet, my waste can, my basket, my stool . . . . First time I've used it for a stove, though, and I suppose I'll have to get me a new one after that." He reached around for his medical bag, then searched through it for matches.

Zeke tried hard to stay awake himself. Maybe the doc's brain was beginning to shut down. He'd never heard of anybody building a fire inside an automobile before, unless he wanted to blow himself up. And while he felt half near death himself, he surely did not want to end his life in fumes and flames.

"I'd go easy there, Doc," he said.

"Give me one of those paper sacks back there, Zeke," Doc Sterling replied. "Just empty it out on the floor—I don't care what's in it." Zeke did as he was told and handed the sack to the doctor. "Now, start tearing one of those cardboard boxes apart and hand me a piece at a time."

The doctor lit the paper and added a piece of cardboard. As flames shot up and smoke curled from the can, he rolled his window down a fourth of an inch and instructed Jesse to do the same. The wind whistled through the openings, covering the doctor's head and shoulders with a fine layer of white. Jesse's, too.

When the paper sack was gone and the cardboard as well, the doctor asked for his medical journals on the backseat. He handed one to Jesse. "Start tearing out the pages," he told him, ripping one out himself, crumpling it up and dropping it into the can where it was swallowed up in flame.

"I'm so cold, Dad, I can hardly move my fingers," Jesse said.

"Keep tearing," his father said.

The heat wasn't much, but it was something, if only to make the inside of the car a bit more comforting, add light to their faces. Zeke studied them from the backseat—the first time that night he could see their eyes, their expressions. Jesse looked so young—still had baby fat around his cheeks and jaw. Zeke had robbed this kid of a mother. They must hate him worse than poison. He wouldn't even attempt to warm himself by their fire. But the fire bothered him.

"Oh, that feels so good," Jesse said, holding his hands above the can.

"Don't know that a fire's such a good idea," Zeke ventured to say.

"Shut up! Just shut up!" Jesse said suddenly, turning on him. "My dad knows what he's doing."

Zeke leaned back again and closed his eyes. "It's all the same to me," he said.

Doc Sterling turned off the flashlight now that there was a small fire going, and Zeke could see smoke curling momentarily up from the floor before it was sucked out a window by the wind. Didn't make any sense at all to light a fire to make it warmer, only to lower a window to let in the cold. But it wasn't his car, so it wasn't his call.

"Keep ripping out pages, Jesse," his Dad said. "Crumple them up and drop them in the can, but don't let your mittens catch."

The sound of tearing pages . . . paper being crumpled . . . the whistle of the wind . . . murmurs from the boy and his father. Zeke closed his eyes and was in and out of sleep. His feet were hurting a little more, though.

He must have slept, because he woke suddenly to find another person on the seat with him. Doc Sterling had crawled back, bumping Zeke with one knee, and was awkwardly sorting through the stuff on the floor, looking for things to burn, tossing them forward along with the cracker box, minus the crackers. Shoelaces, cotton from his medical bag, an oily rag—instructing Jesse to put them in the fire. The oily rag gave off the most heat, but it soon burned like all the rest.

When there was nothing left for kindling, Doc Sterling told Jesse to roll the windows back up. In the backseat he searched until he found a can of car wax. Zeke watched him take his pocketknife and a piece of string to fashion a wick, using the wax as a candle. It gave off light but little heat, and the car grew colder still.

The doctor ordered Jesse to crawl in back with him and Zeke. Soon Jesse was between the two men, and all three huddled together for warmth. There was nothing much left to burn except the clothes on their backs.

"What time is it, Dad?" Jesse asked.

In the glow of the car-wax candle the doctor looked at his watch. "Almost three."

"Do you think . . . if the blizzard goes on . . . someone will come?"

"Of course," Zeke heard the doctor say. *He lies,* thought Zeke.

"But who will know we're here?"

"If Kate was watching for us, she'll know, and she'll send someone."

"What if she wasn't watching, though?"

There was silence for a moment. "Someone will come," was all the doctor said.

Then Zeke heard his own name being called. "Zeke? Zeke?"

He murmured.

"You stay awake now, Zeke," the doctor said.

"I'm so *cold,* Dad," came Jesse's voice.

"I know."

Zeke drifted off and heard himself snore.

And then there came the sound of ripping, tearing, as though they were on a boat, the wind ripping the sails. Zeke did not want to give up his dream of being on a sunny lake somewhere in Minnesota maybe, a fine August day, the sun beaming down on his bare chest, the sails flapping. He opened his eyes, however, to see Doc Sterling ripping open the back of the front seat with his pocketknife—slashing and tearing.

"Dad?" cried Jesse in alarm. "What are you doing?"

"Well, I think we've got about all the good we're going to get out of Gertie, and it's time to say good-bye," the doctor said. "I might forgive her for not having a heater to warm us, but she's going to have to keep us warm with the seat stuffings."

He began tearing at the inside of the seat backs and pulled out handfuls of cushioning which he tucked down around Jesse, like packing material for a box in the mail. A handful for Jesse, a handful for Zeke, more handfuls for Jesse, a few for himself. He tucked them under the boy's chin and around his ears. Then he ripped off the seat coverings themselves and wrapped them around Jesse's legs. When the seats had been demolished, and all possible material had been used to insulate them, he used the smaller pieces to cram around the window glass where the wind whistled through, jamming it up tight with the point of his knife.

They sat as close together as possible, and Zeke began to despair. He did not want to be in this car with the Sterlings. He would have stayed in prison before he went through this. He knew they could have turned him away, could have put him out. Maybe they'd do it yet.

"Well, this is all we've got," the doctor said. "Jesse, you've got to teach us some songs, now. What about that song you sing in school—the air force song?"

"I don't want to sing, Dad," said Jesse in a small voice that made him sound half drugged. His head was leaning unself-consciously against Zeke's arm, and from the weight of it, Zeke knew he was falling asleep.

"Sing, Jesse! You've got to sing. Teach it to Zeke. I'll bet he doesn't know it."

"I can't, Dad."

"*Sing!*" his father ordered.

Jesse didn't even move his head. From down under the blanket, beneath the seat stuffing, a soft voice slowly eeked out the words: "Off . . . we go . . ."

And immediately Doc Sterling picked it up:

> "*. . . into the wild blue yonder,*
> *Climbing high into the sun; . . .*"

Suddenly Jesse stopped singing and his body tensed. Doc Sterling startled and looked down at him. "What's the matter, Jesse?"

And then all three of them heard it—a girl's voice screaming: "Dad! . . . Jesse! . . . Dad! . . . Jesse!"

"Kate!" said Jesse, sitting up. "It's Kate!"

Doc Sterling threw off the blanket and lunged for the dashboard. "The lights!" he said. "The lights!"

Twenty-Nine

She allowed herself to cry a little but kept her mittens over her eyes to prevent ice from freezing on the lashes. There they were, but the rope wouldn't reach! Then she remembered the metal eye on top of one of the pickets. No! It was madness, but it was all she could think of to try. She turned back around and, holding the rope taut, pulled herself along hand over hand until she reached the windmill. She had wanted to go forward but instead she was going back. *Concentrate*! she told herself. *Think*!

Kate untied the rope from the metal framework and, carrying the end of it in one hand, the other end around her waist still, followed the line of pickets back toward the road as far as they went. The third picket from the end, she remembered, had the metal eye on the top. Blindly, snow covering her face, she searched it out, then pulled it from the ground and moved it to the end of the line.

Her breath came short and fast in desperate little gasps as she turned on the flashlight again, held it in her mouth, removed her mittens, and tied the loose end of the drapery cord to the metal loop at the top of the stake. Then she pulled on her mittens again and thrust the picket down, down into the snow until it would go no farther.

Kate faced the road once more, terrified that the car lights may have gone out. But there they were, barely visible now. She started toward them. There would be the fence at the end of the pasture to navigate, and beyond that, the ditch. The snow there could have drifted five feet deep in places. She could see nothing but the dim patch of yellow beneath the snow. Hear nothing but the crunch of her foot-steps and the flutter of her own panicked breathing.

She fixed her eyes on the spot of light. She imagined it was growing fainter. Having lost track of time, she glanced toward the sky to see if there was any sign yet of morning. She had to keep her eyes on the light, she scolded herself. If she lost it, she might never find it again. To be so close now, and to foolishly let her eyes wander. . . .

The snow grew deeper as she approached the fence, and Kate knew it was piling up there. She tried to walk gently, smoothly, keeping one hand on the slack, trailing rope so as not to pull her anchor from the snow. Kate still had to brace herself against wind gusts, and the air was so cold it took her breath away. Ice formed below her nostrils where her nose was running. *Disgusting.*

Almost there, she kept telling herself, repeating it over and over again, the slogan to keep her going. The fact was, how-ever, that she was not almost there, for there was still the fence and the ditch. To her horror, she realized she was walking downhill now, where the pasture sloped toward the road. The blotch of yellow light from beneath the snow ahead was becoming obscured by the ridge of snow rising before her.

"Oh, Dad," she murmured, her breath coming short. "Jesse!" She tried to hurry, wondering if the only way she could reach them was to tunnel her way through the huge drift. But there would be the fence at the bottom of it, and . . .

To her surprise, she discovered she was beginning to walk uphill now. The hardness of the snow enabled her to walk on top of the drift. Gingerly, almost afraid to test it, she put down one foot, then another, keeping her arms spread out to her sides so that if the snow gave way, she would not sink like a rock to the bottom.

But the sheer force of the wind, it seemed, had packed the snow so hard that it held her weight, and she was overjoyed to find, when she reached the top, that she could still see the glow of headlights buried below. She could even see one of old Gertie's rear fenders, and she gave a little cry of delight. As though in answer, Gertie's horn gave a tentative bleat, like a child with croup, and she knew that either Dad or Jesse was trying to signal.

She took a moment to catch her breath. Although the wind whistled and howled around her, exposed as she was on this small hill, she felt almost claustrophobic, as though the snow and the darkness were closing in, pressing against her, crushing her chest.

She took a step downward toward the buried car, and suddenly the snow at the outermost edge gave way beneath her and she was dropping, the snow coming in on top of her. Gasping, she "swam"—pushing the snow away from her face before it could settle around her, thrusting her feet against the leaden snow under her to propel herself forward and down, until finally her head was above the drift and she could dig herself out.

Terrified and freezing, she clawed her way through the snowbank on her hands and knees until she was at last on solid ground. The rope! Desperately she felt for it around her waist. There it was, still secure. Her chest heaved with exertion.

Scrambling to her feet at last, she lurched toward the car. Resting one hand on the snow-covered hood, she ran the other over the right headlight, then stumbled forward to find the left. As the snow gave way she was reassured to see the half-closed lid of Gertie's light.

She braced herself against the car on the passenger side to make sure she did not fall in another drift, and made her way alongside the running board, fighting the biting snow. Running one padded sleeve along the side, Kate searched for the door handle. But the front door was frozen shut. Grasping it firmly, she pulled with both hands until, with the sound of cracking ice, the door opened.

She turned on her flashlight. All she could see at first were torn seat cushions and stuffing, as though a wild animal had broken into the car and devoured its occupants.

"Kate!" came Jesse's voice from somewhere in the dark interior.

Another "Kate," echoed by her dad. "Oh, thank goodness!"

"Dad?" she said, bending down to peer inside. And then her heart seemed to freeze inside her rib cage and she sprang backward.

"*Him!*" she screamed.

Thirty

It seemed to Jesse, groggy with sleep, numbed by cold, that he had been days in the car, squeezed between his dad and Zeke Dexter, and he couldn't quite understand why his sister was screaming. Had she been out in the blizzard all night? Couldn't she find her way back either? He could only stare, for she was covered with snow, her cheeks flaming like the setting sun, the way they always did when she was out for long in winter.

"Kate!" Doc Sterling cried, reaching across Jesse to grab at his daughter. "Crawl in! Crawl in! Jesse, help her!"

"No!" she said, and pulled away.

"You shouldn't have left the house!" her father said. "Get in and close the door."

"You . . . can come," Kate said, but her words were slurred with the cold. Her face looked so strange, the way she was staring, Jesse thought. Had it frozen that way?

"Can we make it to the house? Are you sure?" Doc Sterling said, pushing things on the floor aside so he could get out. In the flashlight's beam, it must have looked as though there had been a tremendous fight, Jesse realized. Maybe that's why Kate had screamed. The only person who wasn't saying anything was Zeke.

"How did *he* get here?" Kate demanded, still looking at Zeke. "What's happened?"

"He was released early and got lost in the blizzard, Kate," her father said as he crawled over Jesse's lap, then Zeke's feet, and got stiffly out of the car. He put out his arms and embraced Kate, but she was near tears, Jesse could tell.

"I risked my life to come out here and find you," she said, "and it's *him!*"

"Kathleen, you're covered with snow and you need to get back to the house," Doc Sterling said. "Are you sure we can do this? I can't see a thing."

Zeke didn't even move. It was as though he had frozen in an upright position.

They left him where he was, and Jesse crawled out after his father, keeping one arm over his face to protect it from the wrath of the wind. Even his father seemed to buckle under the onslaught.

"I've left a trail," Kate said, her voice flat, hollow-sounding.

"Then let's go home," the doctor said.

"What about *him*?" Kate asked sharply, her teeth chattering, pointing to Zeke.

Remembering Zeke, Jesse bent down to look in the car again. But the man still sat half covered with the blanket, hands on his knees, unmoving.

"Jesse," Doc Sterling instructed, "you follow behind Kate, but we've got to hold onto each other. If you lose the hand of the person behind you, stop. We've all got to get back together. I'll come next, and Zeke, you hang onto me."

"Dad!" Kate protested.

"Do as I say," her father said. And then, changing places with Jesse beside the car, he said, "Zeke, you've got to move. You've got to get out now and come with us to the house."

There was a slight stirring within the car, and Doc Sterling leaned forward to help. Everyone seemed to be moving in slow motion, as though there were concrete covering their arms and legs, Jesse thought.

It was difficult to know whether Kate was pulling him or he was pulling Kate. All Jesse knew was that he was so cold he could not trust his legs to bend, his feet to move, his back to support him. He could see nothing and didn't even try, keeping his eyes closed against the stinging snow.

"What are we following, Kate? Where's the trail?" her father called behind them, pulling on Jesse's hand to slow him down.

"I've got a rope," she called back. "It will lead us there."

"Good thinking!" Doc Sterling yelled.

Jesse felt as though he were climbing Mt. Everest. When Kate took a step, he moved. When she stopped, he stopped. They seemed to be going through a tunnel with snow piled high on either side of them. Protected a little from the wind, Jesse could hear more distinctly the breathing of the men behind him, an occasional moan or grunt from Zeke.

"I think we're about there," Kate called back over her

shoulder. "The rope's grown taut. . . ." And then she gave a little cry.

"What?" asked Jesse.

"What is it, Kate?" called their father, alarm in his voice.

'The fence!" Kate cried.

"That's good, isn't it?" said Jesse.

"No! We can't follow it back because there's a whole section missing down here near the road."

"Aren't you following a rope? Is the rope tied to the fence?" Doc Sterling asked.

"It . . . it was tied to a ring on one of Mother's pickets. I stuck it way down in the snow. But here it is, caught on the other side of the fence. It pulled loose, Dad!"

Jesse tried to understand. They had left what protection the car had given them to follow a rope that Kate had tied somewhere, and the something they had tied it to had come loose.

There were tears in his sister's voice when she spoke again, but she sounded determined. "Jesse," she said, handing him something hard and frozen. "You stay right here by the fence and hold onto this picket. The other end of the rope is fastened to my waist. I'm going to take the flashlight and see if I can find the row of pickets I left to get out here. When I do, just follow the rope, and I'll lead you back."

"Kate, if you don't find our way in a minute or two, we'll all go back to the car," Doc Sterling said. "We can't stay out in this. I'm numb."

"Two minutes," Kate begged, and a dim circle of light from her flashlight shone on the snow ahead of them.

Jesse stood pressed against the wire fence, holding tightly

to the picket, feeling the gentle tug on the rope and listening to the crunch of Kate's boots receding on the other side of the fence. His father pushed up against him for warmth, encircling him in his arms.

"Should have brought that blanket with us," was all his father said.

The rope grew taut, then slack, then taut again. And finally, from somewhere up ahead, came Kate's voice. "I found it! I found the row of pickets. C'mon, Jesse! Dad! This way!"

The pickets, the windmill, more pickets again—these almost buried in snow, and then the four of them were crawling through the barn window, stiffly, like wooden soldiers, unable to bend their arms and legs, their clothes crackling.

When they emerged from the barn to follow the wire back to the house, Jesse noticed the first faint streaks of gray in the sky. But better yet, straight ahead, the lamp in the window. He had a sudden burst of energy. He wanted only to propel his frozen body over the doorstep. And then . . . then . . . there they were, going inside. The delicious warmth of the kitchen, the dry chairs, the cake that Kate had baked for them waiting on the table—the wonderful, comforting, familiar pleasures of home. It had never seemed such a palace before.

Hagarty was meowing and scratching from behind the cellar door and Kate let him into the room. The cat shied away from the chunks of snow that fell from their clothes, the puddles of water gathering on the linoleum. Jesse's fingers and toes began to ache and sting, and he could hardly get his boots off. Grabbing all the coats and jackets hanging behind the kitchen door, Kate covered Jesse's back with some of them, wrapping the rest around her own shoulders. Jesse didn't think he would want to take his coat off again, ever. He just wanted to sit there on the chair and smell the cake and go to sleep and . . .

And then the back door opened again, and Zeke Dexter was in their house.

Thirty-One

✳

Zeke was too weak to talk. He had heard the fury in Kate's scream, the hate in her voice. He was aware of the cold politeness when the doctor spoke to him and the reluctance of Jesse to sit beside him in the car. But what little concern he had left for anyone, including himself, was to keep breathing, keep moving till he could just sit down again. To lie down and close his eyes.

Kate and Jesse had gone into the parlor, and Kate had brought the feather ticks down from upstairs. She and her brother wrapped themselves up near the potbellied stove. But Doc Sterling, a blanket around his own shoulders, a stocking cap on his head, guided Zeke down the hall to his office, across from the parlor, and told him to wait. When he came back again, he had an armload of dry clothes, his own.

"These are a couple sizes too big, Zeke, but I want you to change. Come on, I'll help you out of those boots, but I want to have a look at your feet and your fingers. You've got a frostbitten nose, that's for sure."

The doctor was shivering, probably close to hypothermia himself, Zeke thought. He tried to do as the man said, but every movement he made was an effort. Just getting his belt unbuckled was more than his fingers could manage, and the doctor ended up undressing him and helping him step into the baggy long johns and pants that were offered. There was only efficiency and duty in his assistance, but how could it be otherwise?

Zeke's mind went back again and again over the last twenty-four hours, but it got just so far ahead and turned back. There was no going forward because there was really nothing to think on. The house he had shared with Dwayne was gone, there was no place to go, and he had to deal with that.

Sitting in the doctor's big leather chair because he was too weak to climb up on the examining table, his head tipped back, he drifted off into sleep, only to waken suddenly by sharp pains in his feet and find that Doc Sterling had placed them in a pan of warm water.

"It's going to hurt some, Zeke, as they thaw, but how you got through that blizzard with no worse frostbite than this, I'll never know. Fingers are a little worse off, I'd say, but your nose got the brunt of it. Nothing that can't be saved, though, I believe. We'll have to wait and see."

Zeke winced as the aching grew stronger. "I . . . ought to be going. Soon as I get thawed out," he said.

"We'll see." The doctor unfolded a blanket and placed it around Zeke's shoulders. He draped another one over his legs. Then he put a second basin of warm water on the man's lap. "Keep your hands in that," he said.

"It's . . . much appreciated," Zeke said.

Doc Sterling made no comment and left the room. The door stood ajar, however, and Zeke could hear Kate's voice in the parlor across the hall.

"How long is he going to be here?"

"Till he gets thawed out and finds a place to go." Doc Sterling's voice.

"Finds a place to *go*? That's *his* problem! It's a wonder you didn't turn him out in the snow. Why did you even take him into the car?"

"Kate!"

Then Jesse's voice: "Oh, Kate, you wouldn't have turned him away either."

"Oh, wouldn't I? Why didn't you just leave him in the car, then, Dad? The highway crew would find him and take him to the hospital or something. He didn't have to come here."

"Kate, keep your voice down," her father said.

"I don't care if he hears me! Why do you care how he feels? Of all the people who could have been stranded in our car overnight, why did it have to be him?"

Zeke looked down at his feet. They were beginning to feel as though he were holding them over a fire. Just let him get his boots back on, and he'd be out of here. She didn't have to worry about that.

Thirty-Two

Later that morning, while her father and brother and Zeke sat at the kitchen table eating an odd breakfast of coffee, oatmeal, and cake, Kate stood against the wall with her arms folded over her chest. A crackling fire was going in the cast-iron cookstove, and her body had warmed enough to trade her heavy coat for a sweater. But her eyes had not thawed. They were so cold and hard she could feel them boring right through the back of Zeke Dexter's head.

This was not the way she had imagined their homecoming at all—the three of them sitting cozily around the kitchen table enjoying her cake, while Kate told them how carefully she had planned their rescue, the chances she had taken. Everyone was groggy from lack of sleep, and with Zeke there, voices were muted, emotion restrained, and the real story seemed to be how they had survived overnight in the car, not what Kate had gone through to find them.

But then her father said, "Kate, it was a brave thing you

did last night. You took an awful chance, but I don't know how much longer we could have held out if you hadn't found us."

"The biggest chance were those last fifty feet," Kate said.

"That's all it takes, honey. Doesn't even take fifty in a blizzard. Five'll do."

Zeke avoided her eyes and kept them on the small Philco radio Kate's mother had used in the kitchen to entertain her while she cooked or canned or ironed. Jesse and Dad were listening too. Usually they caught the news in the evening, when Lowell Thomas made his commentary. But now news about the storm of March 15 was on every station. What everyone wanted to know, and what forecasters could not seem to explain, was how a blizzard could have blown in with so little warning and on such a mild day. Why had the forecasters missed it, and why, when the warnings did come, had they not been more urgent or precise or consistent?

And no one seemed to know the full extent of it, though cities and towns were mentioned where the storm had passed through—Williston, Bismarck, Devils Lake, Lakota, Grand Forks, Fargo, Moorhead, Thief River Falls. . . .

One guess was that the radio stations had not wanted to interrupt the president's address, meaning that the warnings came too late. Another explanation was that because Canada was already at war with Germany, weather reports from Canada were classified information. But forecasters responded that stockmen had been advised to protect their herds by driving stock to shelter, and that any Dakotan worth the name knew that this meant real trouble was on the way.

Trouble's already here, Kate thought, glaring at the back of Zeke's head.

"What we do know," one announcer said, "is that a high-pressure system from the north met up with a low-pressure area."

"He's got that right," the doctor mused aloud. "Until that storm hit, the wind was from the south. Remember, Jesse? And suddenly the snow and wind were coming right at us and I couldn't see."

"It was more'n snow," Zeke ventured, his hoarse voice barely above a mumble. "Air was full of dirt. Felt like I was choking to death."

Why didn't you? Kate thought bitterly. *Oh, why didn't you suffer even a little of what you did to my mother?*

The sudden ringing of the telephone startled them all.

"It's working again! They must have got the line back up," Kate said. Two long rings and a short, the Sterlings' ring, though they knew that everyone on the party line would run to listen in, wanting to see what news there was of relatives and friends still missing.

Kate lifted the receiver from the hook on the wall. "Hello. This is the Sterlings'," she said.

"Hello, miss. This is Jim Hoverson at the Fire Department. Just wanted to check and see if the doctor got home last night. Got a call from a Mrs. Dryburg, concerned about him. Are you Kate?"

"Yes, and he's here now. He spent the night in the car with my brother, but I went out this morning and brought them in," Kate said, wanting *somebody* else to know and appreciate all she had risked. She was on the verge of saying that there was a sick man there needing transportation into Grand Forks, but her father was already reaching for the phone, and she reluctantly handed it over.

"Dr. Sterling here. . . . Yes, hi, Jim. . . . Looks like it took *every*body by surprise. What's the situation in town? . . . Yes. . . . Yes, I'm afraid so. . . . From the look of things, it could be a week before you plow us out. We've got drifts as high as the porch roof some places."

Standing behind Zeke again, Kate motioned to her father to tell them that Zeke was there. But Doc Sterling ignored her gestures and turned his back to finish the conversation. "I say dig out the folks who need it most. We've got food, got coal. . . . Well, that's good. That puts my mind at ease. . . . Yes, we'll do that. Good-bye."

"They're not going to plow us out for a week?" Kate cried when he hung up.

"Dr. Ingberg is going to see my patients till we're plowed out, Kate. There are still people missing, trapped in their cars. No sense in their spending time sending a plow way out here when we're in no danger."

"I'd think that people might want to know just who is safe and who isn't," Kate said, motioning toward Zeke, unable even now to come right out and say his name.

"Well, nobody knew Zeke was coming home, so nobody's missed him," said her father. "And their phone's been out because of the fire."

Kate grabbed the dishes off the table and plunged them into the sink, not daring to open her mouth again because she didn't trust the words that would spill out.

The radio was giving game scores now for the previous night, and when it came to Grand Forks Central Maroons versus the

Wahpeton Wops, and it was announced that the Wops had won, Jesse gave an anguished howl of disappointment.

"We should have won that one, Dad! We had the players! We should have won!" Jesse kept saying.

"Well, Jesse, there's always next year," Doc Sterling said.

When Zeke left the kitchen to retreat to the blankets the doctor had provided for him, Kate turned to her father. "Just where is he going to sleep?" she asked. She didn't like the sound of her own voice. Didn't like what she had become.

"I expect the daybed in the dining room will do," Doc Sterling answered.

"Well, I still don't know why you didn't tell the fire department he was here. He's got frostbitten feet and hands, you said so yourself. He should be in a hospital!"

Her father was tired, and his voice showed irritation. "I'm a doctor, and I'm supposed to have them send a snowplow twelve miles out here in the country to tend a man I can easily take care of myself?"

"But how can you bear to have him in our house?" she cried.

"Because I have to. There's nothing else to be done. I understand how you feel about him, Kate, but—"

"No, you don't understand, because with you, duty comes first. But I'm a daughter, Dad! I'm the daughter of the woman that he—"

"And I'm her husband," Doc Sterling interrupted. "You're not the only one who misses her. You don't have a monopoly on pain."

His words stung, and Kate's head swam with anger and humiliation and just plain fatigue. She stared down into the dishwater in the basin and scrubbed furiously at the oatmeal pan without really seeing it.

How could this all have turned out so wrong? She'd had no sleep at all the night before and had done what was perhaps the most courageous thing she'd ever had to do. When she had seen the beam of those headlights in the snow, she had been so relieved, so happy! And now it was *Zeke* she had rescued too. Now *he* was in their house, eating their cake, wrapped in their blankets, sleeping on the daybed in their dining room. It was all coming back now, the dreams, the fantasies, the haunting. Unmindful of the dishwater on her hands, she buried her face in her palms and stood a moment without moving. And she thought she had been doing so well.

The telephone told them more than the radio did that Sunday. Jesse went to bed soon after breakfast and got up again in early afternoon, dragging his feather tick with him. It was the first time he'd been warm, he said, and he was going to keep that around his shoulders all day if he had to. But every time the phone rang, they all wanted to know the latest news.

People had spent the night in cafés and churches, friends told them. Twenty women and children stayed in the East Grand Forks fire hall overnight, and the firemen served them lunch at midnight. Highway crews rescued sixty people from stalled automobiles, and there were 150 stranded cars around Grand Forks alone.

Finally Kate, too, took a nap, and when she got up from a restless sleep, she stood at the window at the end of the hall upstairs, and surveyed the frozen landscape, now that the snow had stopped. It was one she hardly recognized.

There were high ridges where the land had been flat, mounds where the pavement had been level. One of the sheds near the barn was buried completely in a white haystack of snow, yet the clearing itself was swept clean in places by the wind, and the bare ground showed through. When Kate's eye spied one end of her father's car out where the road should be, she saw that it had been turned halfway around in last night's gale.

The blizzard had blown out as suddenly as it had blown in, leaving each family to deal with the havoc. It would take some time, but spring was certain. Outside, anyway. Kate faced the bitter realization that her heart had been frozen solid, and spring would come to all but her.

When she went downstairs to join her father in the parlor, Doc Sterling was fast asleep in his easy chair, waking from time to time at some exclamation from Kate or Jesse as they moved about the room, then nodding off again. All the while Zeke lay on the daybed in the dining room, covered with blankets, face to the wall. Whether he was asleep or awake, Kate didn't know.

"Eighty-four miles an hour!" Jesse yelped.

"What's that?" asked his father, jolting awake.

"There were wind gusts last night of eighty-four miles an hour!" Jesse told him, scooting a little closer to the big Atwater Kent dispensing the news. "A plate glass window in the Berg Building blew in, and a WPA shed ended up on the highway near the ballpark! Wow!"

Nancy Barrett phoned Kate around three. "Are you snowbound?" she asked. "Oh, my gosh, Kate, I tried to call you last night but couldn't get through. Isn't it wild?"

"Yes, Dad and Jesse were coming home when the storm

hit," Kate said, and told what had happened, but she didn't mention Zeke. There would be too many questions, and the news would be all over Grand Forks before she even knew what was going to happen herself.

"You are so brave!" Nancy said. "I was listening to the game and had no idea!"

"We lost, of course."

"Isn't it *sad*?"

"How did Tom Harrison do? Did he get home okay?"

"Yes, and he made some of his best shots ever, they said, but it still wasn't good enough, I guess."

"Well, it looks as though I won't be at school for days," Kate told her. "The road's blocked with drifts ten feet high. Except for the telephone poles, you could hardly tell there was a road out there."

"Lucky you!" Nancy said. "You know who else got stranded? The society editor of the *Grand Forks Herald*. She and Mrs. Kannowski had to spend the night in their car, and they only had light clothes with them because they were just at a weekend party or something. They finally wrapped their robes around their heads and ran to the nearest house. She said they joked all night about saving the bluebird on Mrs. Kannowski's hat."

Kate laughed.

An hour later she got a call from Tom Harrison.

"I heard you were worried about me," he said.

"What?" said Kate.

"Nancy said you were sick with worry, wondering if I got home okay last night," he teased.

Kate could hear someone snicker on the party line and figured it was the Finleys' ten-year-old daughter listening in.

"Well, *are* you okay?" Kate laughed, embarrassed.

"Yep. The whole team's accounted for. Nothing hurt but our pride."

It was not until the newscast that evening that the full extent of the blizzard began to be known. "The Red River Valley Blizzard of 1941," one commentator called it. "The Black Blizzard," said another, because all the dirt the wind had blown up had choked people as well as car engines. One man got lost in the storm when he went out to feed his livestock in the barn, and his body was found a half mile away; the principal of Winship School was found frozen to death; another couple . . .

The most amazing story was about the empty twenty-seven-ton Great Northern boxcar that started moving under the force of the high winds. At sixty miles an hour, in near zero visibility, the out-of-control boxcar raced through Northwood, Hatton, Mayville, Blanchard, and Preston before an agent at Hunter threw a derailing switch, bringing the boxcar to a stop. Miraculously it had not hit a single automobile on its wild ride.

Kate served dinner in the kitchen. She put a plate on the table for Zeke only because she knew she would be reprimanded if she didn't.

"I can just take my dinner in the other room," Zeke offered, ill at ease with the family. "Don't want to bother you any."

"You'll be more trouble eating in there. Just sit down," Kate said. She saw Jesse glance at her father, surprised at her rudeness. Doc Sterling studied her over the rims of his glasses.

"You'll eat with us, Zeke. Have a seat," he said.

There were white beans and corn bread and a bowl of applesauce. Kate ate standing up by the window, holding her plate in her hands, her back to the table.

That night the doctor did not try to sleep in his chair in the parlor but came upstairs to his bedroom, tired enough, he said, to sleep for a week. Kate put on her gown and brushed her teeth. Then she sat in front of the big round mirror on her dressing table to set her hair, a glass of water and a tray of bobby pins at the ready. She took a lock of hair and, with a rat-tail comb dipped in water, mositened each lock, twisted it around her finger, then pressed the curl to her scalp and fastened it with a pin. The chore completed at last, her whole head covered with pins, she noticed that the light was still on in her father's room. She hesitated, then put on her robe and tapped on his door.

"Dad?" she said.

"Come on in, Kate," he called.

She went into the comfortable room he'd shared with Mother, with its dark mahogany furniture and the wallpaper with the thin blue stripes and flower motif. "Please don't be mad at me," she said in a small voice, standing there in the doorway.

Her father pulled off his other sock and dropped it on the floor. "Not mad," he said wearily. "Concerned."

"You *know* how I hate him! You know I can't stand having him here."

"'Hate' is a strong word, sweetheart. It's a killer. As bad as any disease."

"That doesn't help, Dad."

"It's hardest of all on the person who does the hating."

"I don't care. It's the only thing that makes me feel alive sometimes—how much I loathe him."

"It's all about forgiveness, Kate."

"No," she said. "That's asking too much."

Thirty-Three

It was strange having Zeke in the house. When Jesse came downstairs the next morning, he did not remember that the man was there until his father said, "Jesse, poke your head in the dining room and tell Zeke I've got some eggs and bacon if he wants any."

"Can't he fix his own?" Kate snapped.

Her father ignored the question. "Or there's oatmeal, if he'd rather," he said.

Jesse opened the door between the kitchen and dining room and found Zeke sitting on the edge of the daybed, arms resting on his knees. He was still wearing Doc Sterling's long johns, a pair of pajamas over them, a blanket around his shoulders.

"Breakfast is ready, Zeke," he said.

The man looked up, hair disheveled, stubble on his cheeks and chin. "Okay," he said. "I'll be there."

Jesse noticed he was holding a small cast-iron replica of a car.

"This yours?" Zeke asked, smiling a little.

"Yeah. It's a 1926 Chevrolet Roadster." Jesse took a tentative step closer. "I've got more," he said, pointing to the window across the room where five other model cars lined the sill. "That orange one with the green top—that was my first one. Yellow Cab Company. Mom gave it to me one Christmas." He went over to where Zeke was turning the car around in his hands, admiring it. "It's hard to find models of all the cars, so I've started a scrapbook, too, just pictures."

"Like to see it sometime," Zeke said. He got up and went down the hall to use the small lavatory off the examining room. When he had dressed, he came out in the kitchen and waited to be invited to sit down. Then he ate quietly, self-consciously.

Outside, in the blizzard's wake, life itself seemed frozen. No birds flew, no snow fell, no cars moved, no children played. Even the wind had lost its breath. The white earth lay stunned beneath a heavy white sky.

Kate had left the room when Zeke appeared, and later, when he took his dishes to the sink, Zeke said to Jesse and the doctor, "I'd like to wash out some of my clothes, you give me soap and a basin."

Doc Sterling pointed to a cupboard beneath the sink. "I expect you'll find what you need in there. You can get to it after Jesse does the dishes. I'm the cook this morning and he's the bottle washer." He excused himself and went down the hall to his office.

"I'll give you a hand, Jesse," Zeke said, and they worked together, Zeke washing, Jesse drying and putting things away. "You like automobiles?" Zeke said finally. "How long has your dad had that Model A?"

Jesse shrugged. "I don't know. Long as I can remember. I think he had a Model T before that." He looked at Zeke out of the corner of his eye, feeling the awkwardness of talking about cars, of all things, with the man who had driven his old beat-up Buick into the passenger side of Mrs. Eggleston's sedan the night she'd picked up Mother and taken her to choir practice. The night only one woman left that car alive. Perhaps Zeke felt it too, because they both lapsed into silence as they moved about the kitchen. Finally the silence seemed even more awkward than the subject, and Jesse asked, "What car would you most like to have?"

"Oh, wouldn't mind having me a Pierce Silver Arrow, but I'd settle for a 1938 Zephyr convertible."

"Only five Pierce Silver Arrows were ever built!" Jesse exclaimed.

"And I put in an order for one of 'em," Zeke said, smiling. "Heard they'll go a hundred fifteen miles an hour."

"Only a racing car would go that fast!" said Jesse.

There were footsteps in the hall and Kate came back into the kitchen. She stopped stone-cold in the doorway, staring hard at Zeke and Jesse doing dishes together. Then she stormed back upstairs and closed her door.

"Don't think your sister likes me much, and can't say I blame her," Zeke said, emptying the dishwater in the sink and rinsing the pan.

For a moment Jesse didn't answer. But finally he said, "Well, I don't like you either for what you did, but I guess I can forgive you. At least Dad says we've got to try. I don't think Kate ever will, though."

"I can live without forgiveness," Zeke said. "I had it to do all over again, I wouldn't be anywhere near that road after drinking. Wouldn't even be in my car. But we don't get to play our hand but once in this life. We've got to take our lumps and live with 'em, and that's all I'm trying to do. Just live with it. But I'm sure sorry."

He washed out his underwear and socks, and Jesse showed him where to hang them on the porch. The heavy pants and shirt he had been wearing when he came hung stiffly on a peg by the porch door. "Those could have stood a washing too, but they'd be a long time drying, and I expect I'll be leaving before then," Zeke explained.

When Jesse went upstairs later to get his scrapbook, Kate confronted him. "I don't know how you can even stand talking to him, Jesse," she said. "I don't want to be near him. It's like . . . it's just not right having him here in our house, eating off Mother's dishes, sleeping on her daybed. That was her favorite place to nap, you know."

Jesse thought about it a minute. "No matter how bad we treat him, it won't bring Mom back," he said at last.

"I *know* that! I'm just staying true to her memory, that's all. How do you think she'd feel, knowing he was here—just going on living his life as though nothing happened?"

"He's been in prison."

"So? And now he's out and he's got a life ahead of him, and Mother never will!"

"So, what do you want to do, Kate? Kill him?" Jesse asked simply.

Kate didn't answer.

Thirty-Four

It was a prison of a different sort. Whenever Kate was around, Zeke felt he had to eat as quickly as possible and leave the table. *Rule #5: After finishing your meal, place knife, fork, and spoon on the right side of your plate. Sit erect; when the signal is given to rise, drop your hands to your sides. At the second signal of the gong march out and to your respective places in a prompt, quiet, and orderly manner. . . .* If he was in the parlor listening to the radio and Kate came in, he felt he should excuse himself and return to the daybed. *Rule #26: At the sound of the 7:30 P.M. signal, all inmates not employed at that time must go to their cell and be locked up for the night. . . .*

In fact, none of the family seemed exactly comfortable having Zeke around, and he spent more time on the daybed than he did on his feet.

The plow might make it there by evening, tomorrow morning for sure, Zeke thought. The minute he heard it out on the road, he was going to put on his jacket and boots, no matter how much his feet hurt, and hitch a ride with the first truck or car that came through. Maybe even the plow driver would take him into Grand Forks.

Just what he'd do when he got there, though, Zeke didn't know. Look up Dwayne, of course. But whoever had taken Dwayne in after the fire wouldn't be in any hurry to take Zeke in as well. He'd need to take the first job that came along.

The calls continued to come in all afternoon, and Zeke could usually make out who was calling: Doc's nurse asking what she should do about a patient; the coal company asking if the Sterlings could get by till Thursday; the neighbor who kept them supplied with ice for the icebox. . . . Zeke heard the doctor say that there was still three feet of snow on his front stoop, and that was probably the only icebox he'd need for a while.

After the last phone call the doctor stood at the door of the dining room and said, "The highway crew says they expect to have us plowed out sometime tomorrow, Zeke. Let me take a look at those toes again."

Zeke obediently took off his socks and let Doc Sterling examine them.

"Still hurt, don't they?"

"Nothing I can't live with," Zeke told him.

The doctor examined his nose next. "I don't know, Zeke. I'd thought for sure you might lose the tip of your nose, but I'm thinking that it may get its circulation back yet. Color's better."

It was later that afternoon when Zeke was trying to wash his hair in the kitchen sink—choosing a time he hoped he would be out of people's way—that Kate came in. He'd just risen from the second rinse and was holding a towel to his head when he saw her observing him in disgust. Then she went to the utility closet for a mop and began vigorously mopping up the small spots of water he had splashed on the linoleum. She came dangerously close to his stocking feet and bumped him with it once.

Zeke turned to face her. "Look," he said. "I don't want to be here any more than you want me here, and believe me, I'm leaving the first chance I get."

"That won't be too soon for me," she replied, and returned the mop to the closet.

Thirty-Five

Her father was right. Her hatred of Zeke Dexter was hurting her more than it was him. It was like bile at the back of her throat, and she felt the need to spit it out at every opportunity.

It consumed her, and as much as she hated having him there, she also felt an underlying satisfaction in demonstrating her loathing. It frightened her, however. At dinner, when the others were seated and she was carrying a pan of boiled potatoes to the sink to drain, she thought how easy it would be to dump the scalding water down Zeke's back. She found herself gripping the handles with both hands and deliberately taking the long way around the table so she would not pass behind his chair. She saw the quizzical look on her father's face, but he said nothing. The potatoes were delivered to the table in a bowl, and no one was scalded. But the satisfaction it had given her just to imagine it left her unsettled.

Was she that depraved? she wondered. It was truly, as her father had said, a sickness, and she began to wonder if she would ever get well. How had Jesse managed to get over it as much as he had? How had her father? How could they sit and talk to Zeke Dexter as though he were a normal human being? What was it that held her back from *living* again? *I didn't get a chance to say good-bye,* she thought desperately, answering her own question, tears at the backs of her eyes. But neither had Dad or Jesse.

They all sat in the parlor later, listening to a local station: "The storm's death toll has now reached seventy-two, and every hour brings new reports of the damage. What we do know is that the Red River valley got the brunt of this storm. . . ."

The snow-blocked roads, they heard, had delayed twenty-five Clay County men from being inducted into the army at Fort Snelling. The storm had crossed into Wisconsin and Michigan, and was entering Pennsylvania and New York. John Moses, the governor of North Dakota, set aside March 23 as a memorial to mourn the victims and honor the many heroic acts of courage that had helped to save lives.

Kate listened with Hagarty on her lap. *I saved some lives,* she thought. *One too many . . .*

When Lowell Thomas's commentary came on later, there was news of a different sort: more bombings, advances, retreats, and casualties in Europe. With all this turmoil and sadness and young men facing the draft, how could she sit here with a cat on her lap and let her hatred of this man consume her? That she hadn't said good-bye was as close as she would allow herself to get to a reason.

Nancy Barrett called to tell Kate that the St. Patrick's Day observance in Grand Forks that afternoon was a bust, and so serious it was hardly any fun at all.

"Tell me something cheerful," Kate said. "I'm fed up with sad news."

"Me too," said Nancy. "Guess we just picked the wrong time to be born."

After breakfast the next morning, with no snowplow in sight, Kate set to work washing some sweaters. She chose the two that were dirtiest, traced their outlines on a large sheet of brown wrapping paper, then washed the first in the sink. After squeezing the water from it, she stretched it out flat on the outline waiting for her on the kitchen table.

Zeke came into the kitchen, where Doc Sterling was pouring his second cup of coffee. Kate noticed that he was dressed in the clothes he had worn when he first came—the stiff, heavy trousers, the flannel shirt—and he was wearing his boots again for the first time.

"Your nose is looking a mite better, Zeke," the doctor said. "Fingers and toes feel close to normal now?"

"They're getting there," Zeke replied. "I appreciate your takin' me in, Doc—everything you did for me. And I would feel better about it if I could do something more to help. If you'll just tell me what needs doing. . . ."

"Well . . . most of the things that need doing can't be done till spring," the doctor told him. "The roof . . . the windows . . . except maybe that pile of tree limbs back there needing to be chopped up. You'd have to dig them out of the snow, though, and pry them loose."

"I think I can handle that," said Zeke.

"Well, then I won't object," Doc Sterling said, walking to the window with his cup, the steam warming his face. He surveyed the snowy mound. "Some of those limbs are awful thick, though. And you've sort of been out of it for a while."

"I've been lifting fifty-pound sacks of flour and potatoes. I figure I can lift a little wood," Zeke replied.

"Okay, then. Ax is in the shed."

The phone interrupted, however, and Kate answered. It was a man's voice.

"Zeke there?" No "hello" or "how are you?" *Dwayne,* she thought. *Obviously Dwayne.* The Dexters had the social skills of a toad.

"Just a moment," she said coldly, and to Zeke, "For you."

He came awkwardly across the kitchen, his boots shedding fine dirt as he came.

"Hello? . . . Yeah, got lost in the blizzard and ended up here. . . . Well, I had good time coming, and they let me out early. . . . So I heard. Lost everything, huh? . . . That old stove?"

Kate pretended not to be listening. She bent over the kitchen table, stretching the sleeves of her yellow sweater so that the shoulders matched the outline on the paper, flattening the neckline.

There was an edge now in Zeke's voice as he talked to his brother. "What do you mean, what do I expect you to do? I just left a message for you with the power company that I was here, that's all. Didn't expect no welcoming party. . . . Well, you didn't let me know the place burned down, neither, so I guess we're about even. . . . You didn't know what to tell me? How about just saying what happened? I'd think that when a man comes home after three and a half years to find his house and everything he owns gone, his brother might have some idea about where he might hang his hat. . . . I'm starting from *zero* here, Dwayne. The ground floor up! . . . I *know* that's my problem, but the house being gone is your problem too. . . ."

There were more words, and then Zeke suddenly put the receiver back on the hook while the voice at the other end was still talking. He went out the back door without a word to either Kate or her father.

Then the phone rang again. Probably Dwayne calling back. But this time it was the highway crew.

"Plow should be out there by late afternoon," a man said. "Had several emergencies closer to town. Just wanted to check and see if the doctor needed anything." Kate handed the receiver to her father.

"Don't think there's a person on Earth who can't live without me one more day," Doc Sterling said genially. "First vacation I've had in years. Take your time." When he hung up, he went to the back door and called, "Just leave it where it falls, Zeke. Jesse can stack it and fill the wood box."

Zeke didn't answer. Just lifted the ax and brought it down hard against the next chunk of wood and the next. Doc Sterling closed the door and went back to his office.

Kate herself was feeling a little better. She was disappointed that the plow would not be out this morning and that she could not be rid yet of Zeke. It meant one more day with him in the house. But she was determined to be more cheerful when she finally returned to school. Try to show more interest in Nancy and Fran. Laugh more. Be a normal girl for once, living a normal life, putting a tragedy behind her.

Out the window she watched Zeke dislodge the first log

from off the pile and drag it to the old stump that her father used as a chopping block. He lifted the double-bit ax over his head and brought it down hard. The piece of limb splintered in two, each half flying off to the side. Zeke placed the next hunk of limb on the block and chopped it, then the next and the next, and the whack of the ax took on an angry sound.

Kate rinsed out her coral sweater next, rolled it up in a towel, then stretched that out too on its sheet of brown paper. She thought of the other kids going to school that morning without her, talking about the championship game at Bismarck, the blizzard. . . . She would miss it all. Maybe she *would* tell them about Zeke when she got on the bus the next morning. At least she'd have something to talk about for a change.

She turned on the little Philco as she worked. A station was playing a recording of "How High the Moon," and Kate sang along.

Jesse wandered into the kitchen. "I wish we could have gone to school today," he said. "I'm bored."

"That's a switch," Kate said. "There's plenty of work if you're looking for something to do. All mine, for instance."

"Like what?"

She tried to hold back a smile. "Well, you could stretch out this sweater for me, rinse out my silk stockings, polish my nails. . . ."

"Uh-uh." Jesse backed away.

"Well, Dad wants you to stack all that wood Zeke's chopping out there and bring some of it in for the wood box."

"That's Zeke out there? I thought it was Dad." Jesse went to the window.

"He's trying to make himself useful," Kate said, barely able to disguise the disdain in her voice. "But don't go out while he's chopping. Wait till he's done."

"I won't get in his way," Jesse said, pulling his jacket off the peg and slipping an arm in one sleeve. He pulled the gray toboggan cap from one pocket and yanked it over his head.

Kate finished stretching her sweater, then rinsed out the basin and placed it back under the sink. She wondered how her mother had ever managed to care for the family. It was all Kate could do to take care of her own needs and get dinner on the table.

Outside there was the *whack* of the ax against the tree limb, the *ker-chunk* of wood hitting the growing pile, a louder *clunk* as Jesse stacked it against the back steps, one piece at a time. It was almost rhythmical, and when the next song came on, "Blueberry Hill," the noises outside became the accompaniment.

Kate had just turned her attention to what she should make for lunch, when suddenly the air was split with a sound she had never heard in her life—whether a curse or a cry or a bellow, she could not be sure, but it was followed by a long, piercing scream.

Jesse!

Thirty-Six

❋

Kate rushed to the door. Jesse stood against the woodpile, screaming. On the ground Zeke lay on his side. A pool of blood under his leg was seeping into the snow.

Doc Sterling came running down the hall.

"What's happened?" he yelled.

Kate could only point, her eyes huge, her throat so constricted that no words came out.

Throwing on his jacket and grabbing Kate's as well, her father burst out onto the porch and down the steps, almost colliding with Jesse, who had turned to run inside. Because her father had taken her coat, Kate thought she was to follow. She ran out on the porch after him, down the steps, and over to Zeke.

His face was white and his eyes wild. One hand was extended down toward his ankle, and his foot was turned at a strange angle. Awful sounds came from his throat, low pitched and guttural.

Instead of giving Kate's coat to her, however, Doc Sterling slid it under Zeke's head.

"Easy, Zeke. Easy," he said.

Kate stood a few feet away, one hand over her mouth. Jesse had stopped screaming now and was crying instead. Everything seemed to be happening on a stage, a group of actors going through a rehearsal, except that Jesse was crying for *him,* and she didn't know her lines.

There was a gash in Zeke's pant leg, and Doc Sterling took his hands and ripped it wider still. From where she stood, Kate could see a gaping wound, blood soaking the pant leg.

"Oh, good Lord . . . ," Doc Sterling murmured, more a prayer than an exclamation.

"When h-he brought the ax d-down, he missed, and it went right into his leg!" Jesse cried, his breath coming fast. "He cut off his foot!"

"Well, not quite," his father said. "Kate, clear the kitchen table, and cover it with a clean sheet."

She didn't move.

"Go!"

Kate turned toward the house as her father yanked off his suspenders and wound them around Zeke's thigh. "Jesse, help me carry Zeke inside," he said.

Still unable to speak a word, Kate rushed back into the kitchen. She pulled her sweaters off the table onto a chair and dashed to her father's examining room for a clean sheet.

It helped to be told exactly what to do. She could not have trusted herself to act on her own. Each moan from Zeke as he was placed on the table brought an unspoken *Yes!* to her lips. How desperately she had wished it. Yet each *Yes!* brought a rebuke for the satisfaction it gave her.

She watched her father cut off the blood-soaked trouser leg and throw it to the floor. Clumps of dirtied snow and mud fell from Zeke's boots.

"Get that cat out of here," her father said suddenly. Hagarty was standing on his hind legs on a kitchen chair, one paw up on the table, looking inquisitively about him. Kate scooped him up in her arms, rushed him upstairs to her room, and ran back down. She washed her hands, tuning out Zeke's moans.

"Jesse," the doctor said, "take off Zeke's boots and socks. Then wash your hands with soap—fingernails, elbows, everything." While he was talking, he dipped up a tin pitcher of hot water from the stove reservoir, mixed in some cold from the pump and, sliding a pan under Zeke's leg, poured the water gently over the wound, cleansing it of blood and sawdust, coloring the water in the pan. Zeke moaned again and jerked his leg. Then, still talking to Jesse, the doctor said, "Come hold this towel right where I've got it against his ankle. Kate, put a rubber sheet over my examining table and pull out the extension."

Zeke tried to sit up on the table, but Doc Sterling held him down, his other hand restraining his legs.

"Don't cut it off!" Zeke bellowed. "Don't cut off my foot! Lemme keep my foot!"

"Easy, Zeke. Nobody said anything about cutting. I've got to get in there and see what damage you've done," the doctor said.

Zeke lay down, his back arched, body tense. Doc Sterling wrapped his fingers around Zeke's wrist and took his pulse.

Kate went down the hall, terrified because the nurse was not there to help. She had assisted her father only twice before when Mother was sick and Nurse Everett was away. Once she had helped deliver a baby and once she had helped set a broken bone. But now there was no one but herself and Jesse, and the man for whom she had wished a terrible death was lying at their mercy on the kitchen table.

She prepared the room, pulling out the extension at the bottom of the examining table, covering the table with a rubber sheet. She got out her father's surgical robe, his mask and cap, the powdered gloves in their sterile container, the sterile instruments in their covered tray, and the magnifying glasses her father clipped on over his everyday specs.

When she went back to the kitchen, she found that her father had cut off Zeke's trousers completely and removed his long johns. Zeke was lying on the table in his underwear and looked strangely thin and white under the kitchen light.

"Okay, Jesse, Kate. I'll get his arms, and the two of you lift his legs gently and help carry him down the hall to my office," the doctor said. "And we need to close the kitchen door behind us."

Why was that? Kate wondered. *Don't think, just obey,* she told herself.

When Zeke was on the examining table, Kate covered him with a sheet up to his chin, tucking the bottom edge in just above the wound so that his face and his foot were all that were exposed.

Her father took a can of ether and punctured a pin-sized hole in the top, just large enough to insert a pipe cleaner for a wick. Then he took the metal face-mask frame and placed layer after layer of gauze over it until there were fifteen layers in all. That was why they had closed the kitchen door, Kate realized. Because ether was so flammable.

Doc Sterling went into the lavatory and scrubbed his hands and arms up to the elbows. He took a brush and vigorously scrubbed his nails. Kate washed too and put on gloves. Then she helped her father put on a surgical robe over his clothes, a cotton mask, the magnifying glasses, and the sterile gloves. All the time her heart was pounding painfully in her chest. *Don't think, don't think. . . .*

"Okay, put on masks, both of you. Then put a pair of gloves on Jesse, and give him a retractor." Kate obeyed, but Jesse looked positively terrified.

Maybe they shouldn't be doing this. Ordinarily her father would have insisted that someone drive an accident victim to the hospital in Grand Forks—call the emergency number.

"Dad," she protested. "Shouldn't we call . . .?"

Even Jesse knew the answer to that one. "Kate, they can't get through!" he said. "By the time they plowed their way out here, he might . . ." He stopped with a look from his father, the tired eyes talking to him above the mask.

While Kate washed her hands again and put on gloves herself, the doctor spoke to Zeke. "Okay, now. Kate's going to give you a little ether because this will hurt and I've got to have you absolutely still. It'll just put you out for a little while till I can get you back together."

"Don't cut it off, Doc," Zeke said again as Kate's father fitted the mask over Zeke's nose and mouth, and all Kate could see of Zeke's face when she came over were his eyes, fearful as he studied her.

Kate stared back, then turned away, both frightened and

fascinated by the power this gave her. Like the Roman emperors—thumbs up, he lived; thumbs down, he died—she knew that he knew death was possible.

"Jesse, you stand over here by me," the doctor said. And then to Kate, "You've seen me do this before. Hold the mask there with your fingers spread. . . . That's right. Now, pick up the ether can in your other hand. Tip it until you get a drop coming off the end of the wick. . . . Yes, just like that. Drop it onto the gauze between your fingers of the other hand, about one drop per second to start."

Kate had watched her father do this before when a woman had a baby, but she had never administered it herself.

"Okay, Zeke," Doc Sterling said. "You just relax now. It's going to take a little time before you feel yourself drifting off."

There was no answer. Only the pleading look in Zeke's eyes.

"Don't take if off, Doc," he murmured again indistinctly from under the mask.

"Another drop, Kate," said the doctor. And after a while, to Zeke, "You feeling a little sleepy now?"

Zeke's eyes began to close, but he didn't answer.

"Kate, I want you to stand right there behind his head and watch his chest. If he coughs, gently lift the mask and let him take one or two breaths. After he goes to sleep, he'll go through an excitement stage and his body will be restless and twitch. But after that, he'll go into a deeper sleep and his breathing should be slow and deep and steady. Very steady. With the same hand that's holding the mask, tip his head back a little to keep his airway open. I wish he hadn't had breakfast this morning . . ." Doc Sterling paused. "If his breathing becomes irregular or shallow, let me know. Do you understand, now?"

"Y-yes."

The doctor motioned her to give the ether a little faster. She tipped the can some more. Two drops at a time. . . .

Zeke appeared to be falling asleep, and for a few minutes Kate was sure he was ready for her father to begin. But then his body grew restless; his arms and legs twitched and his eyelids fluttered. She continued the drops. The hand administering the ether grew cold and she carefully switched hands.

"I'll just do some more cleaning up in that leg while I'm waiting for him to be fully anesthetized," Doc Sterling said. He showed Jesse how to hold the wound open with retractors. He flushed the wound with water from a sterile turkey baster, then cleansed it with antiseptic and delicately began picking out small pieces of sawdust and wood splinters with his tweezers. He bent low, working quietly, intently. In the silence of the room, Kate and Jesse studied each other over their masks.

At last Zeke's twitching stopped. The doctor studied his patient's chest and saw that the breathing was slow and deep and steady.

"Okay," he said. "Let's see what we've got."

His gloved fingers probed inside the leg, and each time they came out, they came out bloodied.

Watch his chest! Kate told herself. *In and out . . . in and out . . .* How easy it would be to give him a little too much, just tip the can when her dad wasn't looking. Was she *mad?* How much was too much? Her heart raced again and she clamped her teeth together to make them stop chattering. His breathing would probably slow and then . . . after a while . . . stop. But she could wait . . . and wait . . . and then she would say in alarm, "Dad, he just stopped breathing!" Just like that. She sucked in her breath in panic. This was terrible. How *could* she?

Zeke's eyes fluttered. He gave a slight twitch.

"A little more, Kate," her father said.

She tipped the can again.

Doc Sterling was talking now, more to himself than to her and Jesse. "I'm trying to see. . . . He didn't get the fibula, but he pretty near hacked the tibia in two. . . ." And then, "Son of a gun, he cut a tendon."

In . . . out . . . in . . . out. . . . Kate suddenly realized that she was pushing down too hard on the mask over Zeke's nose, and she relaxed her fingers. Once again she switched hands.

Doc Sterling probed some more, this time looking out the window as he did so, as though better to concentrate on what his fingers were feeling. Then he peered down into the wound again and shook his head.

In . . . out . . . in . . . out . . .

"Kate," said her father without looking at her.

She dropped more ether onto Zeke's mask. What if she were to give him barely enough? Not enough for her father to notice, perhaps, but enough for Zeke to feel some pain? A drop every five seconds, maybe.

"Check his pulse, Kate."

She did as she was told and reported the results.

"Okay. Watch his breathing, now. Keep those drops steady."

This time, feeling guilty because she had even considered making him suffer, she gave five or six drops at a time, then watched, terrified, for fear it might stop his breathing. She should not be doing this! Dad shouldn't have asked her.

"What are you doing now, Dad?" Jesse asked curiously, shifting his weight to the other foot. Kate could see that Jesse's hands were getting tired, holding the retractors.

"Just compressing the ends of the small blood vessels so I can see what I'm doing here," Doc Sterling answered.

"So, what do you think?"

"I'm thinking I won't have any problem setting the bone, but getting that tendon back together's not going to be easy. Only had to do this a couple other times I can remember, and the results weren't all that pretty."

More sponging of the wound with antiseptic.

"Well, nobody's going to see his ankle much," Jesse said. "Who cares if it's pretty?"

"What I mean is, will the leg work? Will he be able to bend his foot up and straighten his toes? I don't know. . . ." Kate's father seemed to like to talk while he worked. "More than that, can he get through this without getting an infection? And if sepsis sets in, we've got big trouble."

So there was hell to go through yet, Kate thought. Zeke wouldn't get through this so easily. What if her mother had had a doctor handy when *she* was hurt? Kate could tell by the way her father's face tensed that delicate work like this was difficult for his stocky fingers. He was a family doctor, good at peering into ears and inspecting tonsils, at setting bones and listening to hearts and lungs, but reattaching a tendon strained his skill.

"Yes, sir, this is a little bit more than I bargained for," Doc

Sterling murmured. "Problem is, that tendon's retracted way up into his leg . . . and . . . I've got to go up there and find it." His fingers probed some more, and he shifted position, bending down and taking another look, his fingers twisting, pulling. "Tendons are difficult to heal because they don't have a good blood supply. . . ."

The work went on, slow and tedious.

"Yep," the doctor said again. "More than I bargained for." But at last Kate could tell that he was finishing up.

"I don't want him out any longer than he has to be," he said to Kate. "Hold off on the ether now."

And so Kate stood and watched, and after the wound had been sprinkled with sulfa powder, the leg was sewn up and braced with a splint. Zeke stirred a bit, and Doc Sterling and Jesse rolled him over on his side so that, should he vomit, he wouldn't choke or inhale it into his lungs. Kate was no longer needed. She sat limply down on a chair, and her father, thinking the ordeal had been too much for her, let her be.

Suppose she *had* just let him die, she wondered, even though she knew she could never have done it. Even *if,* it wouldn't bring her mother back. Even if she had caused him to suffer even a little of what her mother must have felt, Ann Sterling was gone forever. And for the first time Kate came to terms with the fact that there was no way—*no way*—she could ever get even with Zeke for what had happened.

The plows came in the night. Kate got up and tapped on her father's door around midnight.

"The plows are out there, Dad," she said. "Shouldn't we have somebody take Zeke to Grand Forks?"

The doctor was not pleased to be wakened. "Zeke's not going anywhere, Kate. He was at our house using my ax at my suggestion, and I can take care of him myself," was his gruff reply.

After that the house grew quiet, but Kate did not sleep.

The day that followed and the day after that, the temperature gradually rose and there was a constant trickle of water as the huge snowbanks began to melt and slide away. Here and there a dead sparrow dotted the snow, blown, perhaps, from its nest during the storm. The men who were late getting inducted into the army went to Fort Snelling; the mail that had not been delivered got through. A couple loaned Doc Sterling the use of their car till he could look for a new one, and the highway crew towed old Gertie to a lot in Grand Forks and left her there.

The doctor said he would never again have a car without a radio or heater, and Jesse daily came up with suggestions. "How about a Packard, Dad? A Buick Century?" he asked, eager to go into town with his father some Saturday and visit a showroom.

But Kate did not share his eagerness. She avoided the dining room, where Zeke was recovering, groggy from codeine. Mrs. Everett, the nurse, arrived mornings now to take over his care before office hours began. In the evenings Kate wordlessly took him his meals until he was able to get around on crutches. Then he joined them in the kitchen at dinner. Whether she was upstairs or in the parlor or working out on the porch, the *thud, thud* of Zeke's crutches on the floor told her when he was awake, where he was, until she knew his habits by heart.

She accepted his presence now as punishment for the thoughts she had entertained about his death. When Jesse talked of having a new car, she was more reluctant than ever to drive it, for fear she might actually see Zeke some- day walking along the road. And then she dreamed not that she had run into him, but that she had opened the trap- door on the cistern and seen his face—white and bloated—staring up at her from under the surface of the water.

Everyone, Mrs. Carpenter and Mrs. Kolstad included, seemed to accept that Zeke was there, and treated him with dignity if not affection. Dwayne purchased some clothes for his brother and brought them by, visiting briefly with Zeke in the dining room. And of course the kids at school knew that Zeke Dexter was staying at the Sterlings'. There were no secrets in houses on party lines, and the word would have spread even without Mrs. Carpenter's and Mrs. Kolstad's gossip.

"How can you *stand* having him there?" Fran Moss asked Kate once.

"Well, we're not one big happy family, I can tell you that," Kate said.

The grizzled man slept a great deal of the time, and Kate had the suspicion that he pretended to be sleeping sometimes just to avoid having to talk to anyone. She was cleaning the dining room once when Zeke asked her father, "Just how long you figure it'll be before I can stand on my own, Doc?"

She was horrified to hear her father say, "Well, an injury like that usually takes six to eight weeks to heal, Zeke. Maybe longer. If it gets infected, of course, all bets are off."

Eight weeks and maybe longer? Kate could see the spring

months disintegrating before her eyes. She stoically gathered up Zeke's discarded laundry to take to the porch.

"I won't stay here a day longer than I have to," Zeke said.

"All in good time, Zeke. All in good time," the doctor said.

Was her father keeping Zeke there on purpose? Kate asked herself.

"Dwayne tells me they're needing turkey pickers at Swift over in East Grand Forks. And they might be needing someone at the coffee company. Some of the men there have been called up for the army. There's rooms for rent out that way," Zeke went on.

"Well, that's something to look into then, isn't it?" Doc Sterling said.

Thirty-Seven

Jesse was the one who talked with Zeke when he came home from school each day. Kate wasn't rude to him now the way she had been, but she was cold, Jesse thought. Like she was a hundred miles away. When she wasn't doing homework or working around the house, she took down the tin tray from the shelf above the mantel, carried it to the dining room table, and worked some more on the bridge, determined, it seemed, to make Zeke watch; to be reminded daily of her mother. Perhaps it was her way of showing Zeke that the dining room didn't belong to him; he was not a permanent guest. As soon as she noticed his clutter of liniment and bandages piling up on the table, she removed it to a stand in one corner and brought Mother's handiwork down to take its place.

She did, however, allow Jesse to do his homework at the other end of the table, and as the three of them shared the room, Zeke attempted several times to engage Kate in conversation, but it rarely worked.

"She sure put a lot of work in on that bridge," Zeke said one evening as Kate struggled with one of the supports holding up a suspension cable. "Your mom, I mean."

There was no answer.

Jesse looked up from his math problems. "She had a pattern she was following. It's really complicated. I could never do anything like that."

"She *designed* the pattern, Jesse. She didn't just get it out of a magazine or something," Kate corrected him. "It's an original work."

"Makes it all the more special, then," Zeke said. "I couldn't do anything like that either. Not an artistic bone in my body."

Kate seemed peeved that she had been drawn into the conversation. She worked a while longer and then, as if to signal the session over, picked up the tray and carefully returned it to the shelf in the parlor.

"She sure will be glad to see me gone," Zeke said from the daybed after Kate had left the room. He sighed. "Not any more glad than I'll be, though."

"If your brother can't take you and you can't find a room, have you got any friends you could move in with?" Jesse asked.

Zeke scratched his ear. "Oh, there are a couple of fellas, but we're not exactly close. Guess my family sort of grew up not needing anything from anybody."

"Well, that's lucky, I guess," Jesse said.

"Maybe."

For a long time Zeke lay staring out the window while Jesse worked away at his math assignment. "Only problem with not needing anybody is that nobody needs you," he said at last. "Learned that in prison. Told myself there wasn't a solitary person I missed, locked up in those four walls. . . . Oh, I missed my freedom and a good barbecue sandwich and a bar on a Saturday night, but not one person I felt I couldn't live without. And then, when I come out—on the bus ride home, I guess—I realized there wasn't one solitary person missing me. Just never was on those kinds of terms with anybody. Dwayne's the same way. We take after Dad, I guess. Funny how you can go your first twenty years thinking this is the way everybody lives their lives, and then you look around you someday and you wonder just how different you really are."

"Well. . . . I guess I like you," Jesse said finally.

Zeke smiled just a little. "I sort of like you, too."

But Jesse didn't smile. "You ever going to drink again?"

"Well, now . . ." Zeke rolled over on his side and looked at him. "To be truthful, Jesse, I can't promise you I won't."

"Well, why *not*?" Jesse said indignantly.

"Much as I'd like to, I can't promise I won't take another drink, but I sure won't drink and drive."

"Well, if you ever do, I won't ever, ever like you again. If I ever hear you did that, Zeke . . ."

"I think I can promise you I won't," Zeke said.

Thirty-Eight

The full moon was waning, but Zeke could see its crescent shape through the window by the daybed. The stars were out too, but they were mere pinpoints of light through the glass.

He couldn't figure out what had got him jabbering away like he had that night with Jesse. Said things to Jesse he'd never told anyone, not even himself. Probably because Jesse was still a kid. Zeke hadn't been around kids much; Dwayne never married either, so there weren't any nieces or nephews. Kids just said whatever they were thinking, and Zeke could handle that. It wasn't hidden behind glances and stares and a voice as cold as Alaska.

With Kate it was a different story. The hate she felt for him was like a sore that never healed—her tone of voice or the short answer he got when he asked a question. Mostly the way she didn't answer at all. And Doc? Doc he couldn't figure. Maybe when you were an M.D., Zeke guessed, you had to cope with every kind of creature, no matter how low-life he was.

The doc had been kind enough in the past the few times he'd seen Zeke, and he'd sure been generous now. But he was going to be a lonely man for the rest of his life, perhaps, because of the accident, and that fact was like a wall between them that would always be there. Zeke understood that. You could peek around it or over it, but you could never get to the other side.

He fell asleep thinking how if he ever *did* find his way to the desert and start a little ranch someplace—have a few horses maybe—he could invite Jesse and his dad to come out for a week and ride. But that was like wishing for a fire truck when he was five. The birthday party he'd wanted when he was ten. A girlfriend—yes, he'd even wanted that once—when he got to be twenty or so but was too uncomfortable with girls to search one out. And here he was, almost twenty-nine, dreaming about things that would never happen. He turned over on his side, his back to the moon.

Thirty-Nine

Zeke probably tried to make conversation with her because he had nothing else to do, Kate thought. He couldn't escape her presence if she was working at the dining-room table and he was lying down. She answered him in monosyllables, if at all. She couldn't help herself. He had brought all the old feelings back by coming here. *She* certainly hadn't invited him.

"So how's it going?" Tom Harrison asked her on the bus one morning in April.

"Having Zeke there, you mean? About as awful as can be expected," Kate replied.

"When will he be able to leave?" Nancy wanted to know.

"Not till the middle of May, probably."

"I'll bet he'd rather be any place in the world than at your house," said Tom.

"Why would you care what *he* feels?" asked Nancy. "The more miserable he is, in my opinion, the better."

"Hey! Hey!" Tom put his hands up in surrender. "I'm just

saying, if it was me having to stay with a family when I'd done something awful . . ."

"He can never feel as bad as they do, not if he lived a million years," said Nancy.

"Anyway," Kate said, eager to change the subject, "as soon as he leaves, I'm going to have a party. You can all come and we'll celebrate."

"Now, *that* sounds like the old Kate!" Nancy said approvingly. "Do you remember that birthday party your mom gave when you were nine? A neighbor brought a pony over and took us all for rides around your pasture?"

"And I fell off trying to get on," said Tom, and they laughed.

"Gosh. That seems a long time ago," Kate admitted.

"It *was* a long time ago," said Nancy.

Near the end of the month Kate spent one whole weekend working on the bridge. With prospects of Zeke leaving within a few weeks, it seemed a time for getting things done and moving on. Inwardly she did not feel as confident. It was as though her head was saying, *It's time,* and her heart was pleading, *Unfinished business.* It was time for closure, but something had its foot in the door. If she could just complete the bridge for her mother, she thought—when the last toothpick and broom straw were in place—perhaps it would set her free, make her normal, make her whole.

She worked in silence at the dining-room table, covered now with bits and pieces of her mother's creation. When the project was complete, according to Mother's diagram, with all three sections in place, it would be a delicate masterpiece of arched supports and wispy webbing. Except that Kate could not seem to get the supporting cables to hold, the longer broom straws that extended from the main cable to the floor of the bridge. Once, when she managed for the first time to get them all attached and holding in the first section, the section itself came down, bringing the cables with it, collapsing in a heap on the tray.

"This is impossible!" she cried aloud, a choke in her voice, and was immediately embarrassed for letting Zeke see how vulnerable she was.

He said nothing, however. He was reading a *Saturday Evening Post* and glanced up at her impassively.

Kate shoved away from the table, picked up the tray, and returned it to the shelf in the parlor. She wanted this over with! For every two steps she progressed, the project took her three steps back, it seemed. She was *trying* to move on with her life, as everyone said she must, but things kept getting in the way.

When she went back in the dining room to pick up the pieces of toothpick that had scattered on the carpet, she stumbled over one of Zeke's boots lying half hidden under a chair.

"Would you just keep your things out of the way, please?" she exploded.

And Zeke, irritated in turn, answered, "Well, excuse me for living!"

Yes, Kate thought. That was about it. It was his living that bothered her.

And suddenly Zeke cut loose too. "Look! What do you want from me? I'm sorry! I did my time. I sat in prison for three and a half years because of what I did, and know I can never bring her back, but what can I do?"

"Nothing," Kate replied coldly. "There is nothing at all you can do that will ever make it right."

"So I should just crawl in a hole, maybe, and pull the dirt in over me?"

"Something like that," she said, surprising even herself with her hatefulness. But then she turned on him again, angry tears in her eyes. "Do you have any idea what it's like for a girl to grow up without a mother? It's not as though she was sick for a long time and I knew she was going to die and could get used to the idea. It's like one day she was here and the next she was gone, and I never got to tell her . . ." She choked on the words. "I never . . . got . . . to say good-bye."

He was quiet a moment, taken aback by the glint of tears in her eyes. "No," he said finally. "I don't know how that is, and there's no way I could. But ever since I came, it's like you ball up all your discontents and throw 'em at me."

"So?" she demanded. "Who *else* is to blame? What do *you* know about anything?"

"I know that you got a life to live with Jesse and your dad, but half the time you're off on the moon somewhere 'cause you can't get past missing your mom. And I know I'm the last person on Earth should be saying this, but it's like you and her were living some fairy-tale, the way you got on, that . . ."

"I don't want to *hear* what you think!" Kate cried. "I—"

There was a noise outside—a loud honking, like geese—and suddenly Jesse came clattering down the stairs, yelling, "Kate! Kate! Dad's got a new car!" He tore past her, stumbling over his own feet.

Kate pushed away from the table, glad for the interruption. Grabbing her coat in the kitchen, she followed Jesse out on the back porch and down the steps, still furious at Zeke.

"A 1939 Mercury!" Jesse was yelping, and there in the clearing between house and barn was a shiny blue car. Unlike Gertie, a square box on wheels, everything about this car was curved—the hood, the windshield. The roof of the car over the backseat was shaped like a bullet.

Kate tried to catch her breath, to exchange fury for delight. "Oh, Dad!" she said finally, running one hand over the shiny grille. The headlights were all one piece with the hood, not sticking out like frog's eyes, the way they had on Gertie. Could she learn to drive it? Did she *trust* herself to drive it?

Her father was standing beside the car now, beaming. "I know you wanted to help me choose one, Jesse," he said, "but one of my patients owns that lot this side of the hardware store, and he said, 'Doc, I got a trade-in I wouldn't let anybody have but you.' Well, I just had to get a look at it, and here it is. Get in, Kate. You're driving."

"What?" she said, but Jesse was already crawling into the backseat, and beginning to smile herself, Kate went around the car and slid in.

"A heater!" she said, feeling warmth on her legs.

"A radio!" yelled Jesse.

It wasn't new, but it still had some of that new-car smell. Compared with the '31 Ford, it looked like the latest thing to roll off the assembly line. Kate had already learned to drive Gertie, but she had never wanted to go out on the road with it, wouldn't even go for her license—afraid, she said, of an accident. A lot of her friends had licenses—

people needed on farms could get one if they could see over the steering wheel, almost. But whenever she'd thought of the road beside the Nortons' barn, and the tree with the crash marks on it . . .

She didn't want to think of Zeke right now, though, just wanted to enjoy the moment. Her father had gone around to the passenger side, so Kate got in the driver's seat. She turned the key and released the clutch, but gave the engine too much gas and the car shot forward, Jesse hooting with delight. She pressed her foot on the brake, and they jolted forward, then back again, all three of them laughing.

Kate steered it around the clearing and practiced backing up by the shed.

"Hey, Kate! You could take me to the rink from now on, and to all the home games!" said Jesse.

"I'd probably dent a fender first thing," she said.

"Oh, I don't think so," said her father. "I'd say you're a pretty careful driver."

"When can I learn?" Jesse asked as Kate drove down the lane to the road. "When I'm fourteen?"

"Now, I expect that'll be a little too soon to suit me," Doc Sterling said. "But we'll probably keep this car for a good long time, Jesse, so your chance is coming. I heard that Detroit's going to turn their factories into defense plants before this war's over. No telling when we can buy a new car again, so we better take good care of this one. Hard to say good-bye to Gertie, though. I saw her there at the back of the lot, her seats all torn up. Sitting there with a whole row of other cars that had come through a lot worse than we did. I'd swear she even winked at me with that half-closed eye."

Kate drove the Mercury a couple of miles down the narrow road to where it crossed the state road, then turned around and came back. When she parked it again outside the house, she and Jesse checked it over—the glove compartment and the sun visors, the radio stations and the windshield wipers. She was glad for this one nice thing to happen after her flare-up with Zeke, and imagined herself driving over to Nancy's sometime, maybe picking up Fran on the way—the three of them going somewhere together.

"I want to show it to Zeke!" Jesse said, scrambling out at last, and followed his sister and father into the house.

Why Zeke? It's as though he's family! Kate thought.

Just as they entered the kitchen there was a crash from the parlor, the sound of tin hitting wood, and a loud *clang*.

Kate gave a little cry. Scarcely breathing, she raced through the dining room to the front of the house. There was Zeke, standing by the window as though he had just turned around on his crutches. And there on the floor, scattered in bits and pieces, was the bridge—the tray overturned, toothpicks and broom straws strewn about the carpet.

Kate gasped, turning instantly on Zeke. But there was a plaintive cry from somewhere in the room, and she looked up to see Hagarty on the shelf above the mantel.

Forty

Jesse stared at his sister there on the rug, crumpled against Dad's easy chair, sobbing—at his father silently picking up half-demolished sections of the bridge and putting them back on the tray. Zeke hobbled over to the shelf and lifted down the young cat, whose tail was thick with fright, having found it far easier to make the leap to the shelf than to find his way down again. He handed the cat to Jesse.

"You bad thing," Jesse murmured to Hagarty. "Just look what you've done."

Hagarty struggled to get down, and when Jesse set him on the floor, he looked at the mess around him, then wandered over to Kate and put one paw on her lap. She pushed him away.

"Well, this is a rotten shame," Doc Sterling said. "You worked so hard on this, Kate."

"So did Mother!" Kate sobbed. "She spent hours and hours and hours on it!"

"I didn't even know the cat was up there. Didn't know he could jump that high," Zeke said. "I was watching you drive the car around, and the next thing I knew . . ."

Jesse stood with his arms dangling, not knowing what to say or how to help. It just seemed to him sometimes that for every good thing that happened—something that could make Kate laugh—something bad happened. He knelt down and began picking up pieces too.

"Well, honey, you tried," Doc Sterling said to his daughter as one sob followed another. "And that's all Ann would have expected you to do. She knew how much you loved her, and—"

"*Did* she? *Did* she?" Kate cried, and then she turned an angry, tearstained face to her father. "How do *you* know that? Don't tell me things unless they're true."

"Kate!" her father said in surprise.

Jesse watched wordlessly as his sister scrambled to her feet and ran upstairs, crying still.

Forty-One

"Kate."

She had lain so still, so long, on her bed, her wet cheek pressed against the chenille spread, that when she rose up, the imprint of the design made ridges along the side of her face.

She put her head back down again without speaking.

Doc Sterling came on in the room, and when Kate still didn't sit up, he pulled a chair over to the bed. "What is it?" he asked.

She kept her eyes closed a moment longer and finally said, "Just don't tell me things that aren't true."

"When did I ever?"

"You don't *know* what Mother was thinking when she died! You don't *know* whether or not she knew I loved her."

"Kate!" Her father reached out and gently brushed the wet hair from her face. "Why do you say that? Why would she doubt?"

"Oh, Dad!" And suddenly Kate curled into a small ball,

her knees drawn up to her chest. "You just don't know! We had . . . we had an awful quarrel that evening before she left for choir practice. You weren't home yet, and . . ."

"Ah." The fingers continued stroking her forehead. "Then, tell me."

"We hadn't been getting along so well all week." Kate swallowed and needed a handkerchief. She took the one her father gave her, and went on: "Just the usual stuff, nothing big. I hadn't done my work for one thing—scrubbing the bathroom—and Mother wanted it done before she had some women in for lunch that Thursday. I didn't do it; I just forgot. At dinner that evening she told me that because I hadn't done it, I couldn't go to Fran's on Saturday, something I'd been counting on."

She stopped, wondering if she could get this out, this secret something that had been clogging her heart.

"'You should have reminded me before I went to school this morning!' I cried. 'You should have given me another chance.' But she wouldn't give in. She said she'd reminded me enough, and that if I didn't do my work, there were consequences."

"And . . . ?" said her father gently.

"Oh, I was furious! If she had told me what the punishment would be, I know I would have remembered to do it. I just . . . I was crying that it wasn't fair, and I should have been warned, and then I screamed at her that . . . that I hated her! And ran upstairs."

For a full minute Kate lay without speaking. Her father was quiet too.

"I knew, of course, that she was right," Kate went on at last. "I knew she'd had to scrub the bathroom herself that day for her guests, along with getting the rest of the house in order. I . . . I opened the door of my bedroom and stepped out in the hall. I was going to come downstairs and apologize . . . and then I heard Mrs. Eggleston's car drive up and realized Mother was going to choir practice. And . . . she left." Kate swallowed again and buried her face in one arm. The next words came out soft and high, like a kitten's mew. "The l-last thing I ever s-said to her, Dad, was 'I hate you.'"

Kate felt that all her pores were opening, all secrets flowing out. That there would be no more tiptoeing around, being careful not to awaken the thought that followed her from year to year, day to day, room to room. . . .

She lay weeping silently now, breathing deeply. The only good thing left in this world, she felt, was her father's fingers against her cheek.

When he spoke again, he recited a poem:

> *"May never was the month of love,*
> *For May is full of flowers;*
> *But rather April, wet by kind,*
> *For love is full of showers."*

"How is that supposed to help?" Kate asked.

"It's a poem your mother and I used to recite to each other now and then. After a quarrel, as a matter of fact."

"A big quarrel?"

"Oh, yes. We had some magnificent rows."

Kate sat up and wiped her face. "I don't remember any."

"Of course not. We saved those for when you kids weren't around. The big ones, anyway."

"How did it help? The poem?"

"It's just a reminder, I guess, that love isn't constant. It's hills and valleys, and sometimes arguments over the stupidest things. But . . . as I said to your mother . . . we always came back to each other and always managed to capture what we had before."

"I said such an awful thing to her, though."

"I know. But I'm sure she heard you open your door."

"What do you mean?"

"If we had had that quarrel, you and I, and you'd run upstairs, and later I'd heard a door open, I'd have known it was you wanting to come down."

"Really?"

"Yes."

"But what if she *didn't* hear my door open? Mother and I never recited that poem. We didn't have an understanding that no matter what we said, we'd always love each other."

"Maybe you didn't know about love then, Kate, but she did. Even if she didn't hear you open your door, she knew about love."

For a long time Kate sat on the bed, her hands limp in her lap. "If it weren't for Zeke and what happened that night . . . I can never forget what he did, Dad."

"No. I suppose not. Neither can I."

"And if I can't forget, I don't see how I can forgive."

"They're not the same."

"Even so, I've *tried*. I've really wrestled with myself, and all I can think of are ways I want to hurt him."

"We're all in this together, Kate, and it's not easy. We're all three trying to find a way to forgive."

• • •

She was quiet in the days that followed. She could, she decided, *act* as though she had forgiven Zeke, even though she hadn't, and perhaps real forgiveness would follow.

With a great effort of will she said "Good morning" to him at the breakfast table and inquired about his leg. He seemed to take each inquiry as her way of asking how soon he'd be leaving, and would answer with the latest progress he had made toward finding a job and a place to live as soon as his leg had healed.

It was when she passed the tin tray and the almost demolished bridge sitting untouched in the glass-front cupboard in the dining room, however—the never-to-be-finished masterpiece her mother had intended—that rage roiled inside her again. It should have, and could have, been kept in there all along. But this time she knew that the anger was against herself. She had known that Hagarty liked to explore. She had seen him jump to high places, though never as high as the shelf. The tin tray protruded out over the edge, and it took only a cat's tentative paw to send it hurtling down. A mistake she would regret forever.

Zeke was usually in the kitchen having his afternoon coffee when she and Jesse came home from school—Kate arriving first, Jesse ten or fifteen minutes later. Doc Sterling took patients most afternoons, and Zeke tried to be out of the parlor then. But he always seemed to be waiting for Jesse, not her. He and Jesse talked about a lot of things. There was only one topic between her and Zeke, and it was better not to bring it up.

But on this particular day the kitchen was empty and the coffeepot still three-quarters full. Perhaps he was gone, Kate mused. Maybe his brother had found a place for him after all and had come by to pick him up. Perhaps the house would be theirs again, just hers and Dad's and Jesse's. And maybe someday she would feel like giving that party she'd talked about, though she doubted it. Or she'd drive the Mercury to town some Saturday, though she doubted that even more.

She hung up her coat and went into the dining room to check, and then she paused in the doorway, her eyes riveted on the table. The bridge was in production once again, two of the three sections resting securely on their supports, each with its main cables strung from post to post. With a look of deep concentration Zeke was slowly, gently gluing a broomstraw supporting cable in place, attaching it to one of the main cables that swung delicately above the floor of the bridge in a graceful sweep.

"Hope you don't mind," he said without looking at her, so intent was he on his work. "But the doc says I'm here for another two weeks, and I figure I might as well be useful. Never tried my hand at anything like this before, but I guess if I worked on clocks and radios, I must have learned a little something." He glanced over at her uncertainly.

Kate's first impulse was to say, "Don't touch it!" But she checked herself and walked over.

"What I did, see," Zeke explained, "was take my pocketknife and put a little notch right there"—he pointed to one of the supports—"and then I notched the section that fits on top of it, so it's not just glue holding them together, you've got a little something more holding its weight. Can't hardly see the notches, so don't think your mom would have minded." He hesitated. "If that's all right with you."

Kate sat down silently at the table and examined his work—as meticulous and dainty as Mother's, but sturdier.

"No," said Kate. "I don't mind."

She watched him then as he tackled something else—the way he glued two pieces together and let them dry completely before attaching them to the rest.

"I was afraid it was ruined," she said at last.

"Well, she left her design, so we know how she wanted it to turn out," he said.

"Yes," said Kate.

He didn't look at her as he worked and she didn't look at him, keeping their eyes, instead, on the bridge. It was easier this way, Kate discovered, than looking someone in the eye.

"Let me know if you need anything," she said.

"It'd be a help if you could take that knife there and cut me a bunch of toothpicks," he said, pointing to Mother's diagram, where there were small rods extending from the pedestrian railing to the floor of the bridge along its whole length.

Kate studied the design. "Cut them in halves or thirds?" she asked.

"Well, you decide and let's see how it works," he said.

Out in the parlor Kate heard her father ushering in his next patient to the examining room, and at about the same time Jesse came bounding in. Kate could hear the door of the icebox open as he clunked his books on the kitchen table. Moments later he appeared in the doorway with a piece of cold corn bread in his hand.

"Hey, Zeke, I . . ." He stopped, staring at Zeke and his sister working side by side. "You're building it back!" he said in amazement.

"Tryin' to, anyway," Zeke told him, smiling. "Don't talk too loud, though."

Kate saw that Jesse's eyes were really on her. He gently pulled out a chair across from her and sat down slowly, as though, as Zeke indicated, any unnecessary vibration might bring down the structure.

"It's looking good," he said. And then, wanting to encourage this truce, he said, "You know what Zeke wants to do, Kate? He wants to start a ranch on the desert and rope wild horses."

"Pipe dream, that's all," Zeke murmured.

"It could happen, right, Kate?" Jesse said.

But Kate was working and didn't answer.

It was a race to see which healed first—Zeke's leg or the bridge.

The leg was doing better, and Doc Sterling said that in another week, perhaps, he could put his full weight on it. He would probably always walk with a limp, but at least he could walk, and by that account, he was lucky.

The bridge, of course, Kate would have to finish on her own, but Zeke said he would do what he could before he left. The war in Europe was heating up. Germany had invaded Greece and Yugoslavia, and the foreman at the Pioneer Coffee Company was losing another man to the draft. He told Zeke he would take him on in June.

The healing most in question, it seemed, was Kate's heart. She could work alongside Zeke now and talk to him as long as her hands were busy. But she could not talk to him as a friend and doubted she ever would.

One afternoon when Kate came home from school, Zeke said, "Mail call. There's a letter for you."

Kate opened the door to the parlor, said hello to Mrs. Everett, who was taking a woman's temperature, and went over to check the mail on the table near the door. There was a new *Life* magazine, a journal for her father, a bill from the coal company, and an envelope for her.

At first glance it appeared to be an invitation, but when she opened it, she read:

> *Miss Kathleen Sterling*
> *invites you, Tom Harrison,*
> *to a party at her home on* _____, *1941,*
> *to celebrate, well, spring.*

And he had enclosed a stamped, self-addressed envelope.

Kate laughed aloud as she took it back to the dining room and read it silently once again.

"Well, I guess it's not a letter from the draft board," Zeke commented.

"No, just a crazy letter from a guy at school."

"You see this guy at school and he writes you a letter? I never got a letter in my whole life. Not a personal one, anyway."

"Well, it's not exactly a letter. He's inviting himself to a party."

"Oh. Didn't know you were having a party."

"I'm not, exactly. I mean, I haven't planned it yet. He's trying to plan one for me." Ignoring Zeke's puzzled look, she tucked the letter away in her skirt pocket and reached for the glue, bending over the work at hand but smiling still.

On the fifteenth of May, Kate came in to find Zeke packed and ready to leave. Dwayne was coming to pick him up, he said, and was driving him to the room Zeke would be renting near the coffee company.

"What you need to do here," Zeke said, showing her one last detail of the bridge before he left, "is to make this support rest a little closer so that it sits partly on the floor of the bridge, isn't just glued to the side. That's the only fault I've got with her design—you can't make the glue do all the work. It'll bond better if it gets something to sit on."

"I think I've got it," Kate said, carefully lifting the tray and closing it up again in the dining-room cupboard, away from Hagarty's attention. Jesse came in right then, and Kate picked up her books and went upstairs, away from the rambunctious children in the parlor who were awaiting their smallpox vaccinations.

She was feeling unsettled and anxious—the way she felt awaking from a dream sometimes. She tried to put her mind on a party, if there was one—what she would serve. They could make ice cream, and each take a turn at the crank. Put ice cream in tall glasses and pour root beer over them to make their own black cows. She could bake a coconut cake. Have popcorn. Maybe she could even drive around and pick some of them up, and the girls could spend the night later after the boys went home.

Her mind raced on ahead, making plans, but once again it was as though someone were applying the brakes, holding her back; there was a foot in the door, so that it never quite closed.

After the last of her father's patients had left for the day and Kate heard Mrs. Everett's car pulling out, there was another sound in the distance, louder and a bit rattling, and Kate knew that Zeke's brother was coming to pick him up.

She heard his truck turn in at the end of the lane and make its way up to the house.

Still holding Hagarty in her arms, Kate went to the top of the stairs and listened. She heard her father's calm, businesslike voice wishing Zeke good luck. She could imagine them shaking hands, her portly father with his glasses halfway down his nose, shirtsleeves rolled up, suspenders over his shoulders. And Zeke, his hair in need of cutting, wearing a fresh shirt and the trousers his brother had brought him, the rest of his things stuffed in a large paper bag.

Zeke would shake hands with Jesse next, and yes . . . there it was. She could not make out what Zeke was saying, because his voice, as always, was low, just above a mumble, but she was pretty sure it was something about basketball—baseball maybe—because it made Jesse laugh a little.

Then the moment of silence she was dreading, and Kate knew they were looking around for her. She ought to go down, but she couldn't. Physically, she could not move her feet. She was not good at good-byes.

"Kate?" called her father. "Zeke's leaving now."

She should make peace with him when she hadn't made peace with her mother? Kate closed her eyes and leaned against the wall. Hagarty squirmed and she let him jump to the floor.

"Don't believe she heard," her father said, and his footsteps came to the bottom of the stairs. Kate slipped back into her room and closed the door. He called again, but he did not come up.

She didn't know what was said at the last. A minute or two later she heard the back door open, footsteps on the porch, and then, from behind the curtain, she saw Zeke walking—limping slightly—across the clearing to Dwayne's pickup truck. He set his bag in the back, then went around to the other side. For just a moment he glanced up at her window, but then he climbed in.

Dwayne gave a wave of his hand to Doc Sterling and Jesse, who were watching from the steps. And then the pickup moved slowly down the drive, rattling as though a part would fall off any minute. The noise of the engine grew fainter and fainter as it reached the road, and after it made the turn, it was drowned out by a plane.

Dinner was a quiet affair, Jesse doing most of the talking. Baseball season had begun, and he wanted to be batboy for the local team. Who did his father think had the best team for winning the World Series? Cincinnati again? And when his father didn't pick up on that, he switched to football. Would Tennessee bounce back to win the Rose Bowl this time? Would the Redskins ever recover from that loss to the Chicago Bears, 73–0? Who would win the Heisman Trophy?

But after a while the fact that Jesse was the only one talking became obvious even to him. At last he stopped and concentrated on the meat loaf that Mrs. Carpenter had placed in the icebox that morning when she came to cook.

Kate ate without tasting. Was she going to go on forever like this? Would this hole in her heart never heal, and would there always be this leak—leaving such a pitiful supply of mercy and forgiveness? She saw the pain in her father's eyes once when she glanced over and found him looking at her. Unable to bear it, she left the table.

She had been civil to Zeke near the last. Even thoughtful at times. She had sat across from him at the dining-room table and worked with him on the bridge. She had cooked for him, even washed his clothes once. Wasn't this enough? She knew why her father had kept him here for so long after the accident: For her sake as much as for Zeke's. But forgiveness seemed too much to ask of her. She could say the words, of course, but she wouldn't believe them, and neither would he.

On the bus the next day Nancy said, "I thought Zeke left."

"He did. He's renting a room somewhere."

"Well, *that* must be a relief," said Nancy. "So, when's the party?"

"Oh . . . soon," Kate said, and avoided Tom Harrison's eyes across the aisle.

In social studies Mr. Kramer stood at the blackboard listing all the countries that had entered the war so far— whether Axis or Allie. Kate felt she could not endure so much conflict, for there was a war going on inside of her.

When she got home that evening, she was standing in front of the icebox, trying to think what to make for dinner, when Jesse came in and slumped dejectedly onto a chair.

"I really . . . *really* . . . did a dumb thing today," he said. "To my best friend, too."

"Sid?"

"Who else?"

"What did you do? Have a quarrel?"

"It would have been better if we had," Jesse said miserably. "I wish he'd just socked me."

"What did you *do,* Jesse?"

Jesse looked chagrined. "We were talking baseball. I said if I ever played for a big team, I'd want to play shortstop. Then Sid said how *he'd* like to play third base, and I said, 'Sid, *you* couldn't play baseball!' Because of his arm, you know—but, I mean, it's so obvious. Sid knows he can't too, but he can dream, can't he? *Why* did I say that?"

"You probably blurted it out without thinking," Kate told him. "Just tell him you're sorry."

Jesse rested his chin in both hands and stared down at the table. "That wasn't the worst. Then Roger said, 'Sure, Sid can play third base.' And I said, 'How?' and he said, 'He can *be* third base,' and everyone laughed. Including me."

He didn't have to explain it further. Kate could already see the grotesque scene in her mind—Sid Green, with his missing arm, lying on the ground as players slid into him like he was an old potato sack.

"And I could tell . . . I could just tell by the way his mouth turned down that even though he was smiling, he was hurt. I really hurt him by laughing."

"Did you apologize?"

"Well, sort of. After lunch, when we were going outside, I said, 'Listen, Sid, I didn't mean . . . ,' and he just said, 'Forget it.' But *he* hasn't, I can tell. I'm just dumb. Thoughtless and dumb."

Kate retrieved some apples from the refrigerator and sat down to peel them. "You're only eleven, Jesse," she said. "It *was* stupid and thoughtless, but you'll probably be extra careful from now on. It takes time to learn to be kind; you don't grow up all at once." She thought of her father's telling her that he and Mother argued occasionally and said ugly things. "Even when you're *grown* you'll still say things without thinking. Just go on being the best friend you can to Sid, and he'll know for sure you're sorry."

Jesse let out his breath. "Okay," he said, looking relieved. "What are you making?"

"Apple brown Betty."

"My absolute favorite," Jesse said, and went into the other room to play with Hagarty. How easy it was for Jesse.

When the dessert was ready for baking, Kate placed it in the oven and went upstairs. She lay on her bed, waiting for the last patients to leave before she made the rest of dinner. Her eyes drifted over to the photograph of Mother on the wall—Mother as that young girl of ten. Kate herself had been only eleven the night Mother died, the same age Jesse was now.

She studied the photograph as though seeing it for the first time. Mother had known what it was like to be ten . . . eleven. . . . She must have known what it was like to be hateful in the heat of anger, too. And if she knew, as she'd told Kate's father, that they would always love each other and come back, she must have known the same about a daughter only eleven years old.

And suddenly Kate realized she could never forgive Zeke Dexter until she had forgiven herself. As long as she was sentenced to guilt and recriminations, she would go on hating Zeke. It was as though she were coming out of a long illness, a painful journey whose destination had been unclear. As though her lungs were breathing in fresh air now, invigorating her body, and her father might say, were she sick in bed, "She's passed the crisis now."

She lay a very long time without moving. She had almost

fallen asleep. But when she got up at last, she went to her desk and took out a sheet of writing paper:

Dear Zeke:

If this is really the first letter you ever received, I guess I'm glad it's from me. Thank you for helping with Mother's project. The bridge looks a lot stronger than it did, and the cables are holding well. I hope your room is okay and that your new job isn't too hard on your leg.

If you are surprised to get this letter, I'm even more surprised to be writing it. Mother's death was something I didn't think I would ever get over, and in a lot of ways I never will. But hating you was making me sick, and it won't bring her back. I just wanted you to know that I forgive you for what you did, and this is probably the hardest thing I ever had to do.

I just hope that because of it, we're both better people. And I hope that someday, like Jesse told me, you get to the desert and rope your wild horses. If you do, write and let us know.

Kate

She sat back and read the letter again, then lingered a while longer, looking out her bedroom window, over the slowly greening countryside. It, too, was coming back to life after a cruel and terrible winter. She thought of the news from overseas . . . thought about Tom Harrison and whether or not the war would still be going on when he was twenty-one. Thought of Jesse . . .

How wonderful and terrible both it was to be alive at this particular time. How precious every moment, every person.

She put Zeke's letter in an envelope with his name on the front, then took out the party invitation from Tom Harrison. In the space provided, she wrote, "June 7."

The last patient had left the house along with Mrs. Everett, and the scent of apples and cinnamon filled the rooms. When Kate went downstairs, her father was rummaging about the kitchen, lifting pan lids, and checking the oven to see if any dinner was in progress.

"It'll take a while yet, but I'll get there," she promised. She handed him the envelopes to mail when he made his hospital rounds the next morning. "If you could, will you fill in that address for me?" she said.

And then, noting his look of surprise when he saw it was addressed to Zeke and the pleasure in his smile, she added, "And guess what, Dad? I think I'm ready to drive."

Literature Circle Questions

Use the questions and activities that follow to get more out of the experience of reading *Blizzard's Wake* by Phyllis Reynolds Naylor.

1. Why is Zeke Dexter getting out of jail? How long has he been there? Where is he going?

2. What is the connection between Zeke and Kate? How does Kate feel about Zeke?

3. What is "the bridge"? Why is it important to Kate?

4. Why can't Zeke reach his brother by phone? What doesn't he know? What problems will this make for him as he heads home?

5. How has Kate been affected by her mother's death? How has it changed her life?

6. List all the ways day-to-day life was different in 1941 from the way life is today. List all the ways it is the same.

7. Imagine you were Jake or Kate during the blizzard. How would you react to the appearance of Zeke Dexter? What would you do? Why?

8. On page 150 Reynolds writes, "Kate faced the bitter realization that her heart had been frozen solid, and spring would come to all but her." What does this sentence mean? What keeps Kate's heart so cold, and what keeps it from warming?

9. War—from President Roosevelt's address to the nation to Kate's history teacher's lectures—is always in the background in this story. What do the war preparations have to do with the story symbolically?

10. Explain the title of the book. What does "wake" mean? What alternative meanings could the title have? What other titles could this book have had?

11. If Zeke had not ended up at the Sterling's house, how do you think Kate's life would have been different?

Note: These questions are keyed to Bloom's taxonomy as follows: Knowledge: 1–3; Comprehension: 4–5; Application: 6–7; Analysis: 8–10; Synthesis: 11–12; Evaluation: 13–14.

12. At the end of the book, Kate writes Zeke a letter. What do you imagine he thinks of it? What do you think he would say if he wrote a letter back to her?

13. Was Zeke sufficiently punished for his crime? Why or why not?

14. Do you think Dr. Sterling should have behaved differently in any way? Explain.

Activities:

1. Get together in a small group and talk about forgiveness. Is there anyone you can't forgive? Why? What was the hardest thing you've ever had to forgive someone for? What was the worst thing you've been forgiven for? Would you have forgiven Zeke Dexter if you were Kate?

2. Research drunk driving laws in your state and make posters for your classroom and school about the dangers of drinking and driving.

3. *Blizzard's Wake* is based on a real event, the Red River Valley Blizzard of 1941. Find some old newspapers from your community and find an event from long ago to use as the basis for a story you write. Combine historical happenings with fictional creations.

Also by This Author:

How I Came to Be a Writer, Aladdin, 2001
Jade Green, Atheneum, 2000
Reluctantly Alice, Aladdin, 2000
Sang Spell, Aladdin, 2000
Shiloh, Aladdin, 2000
Walker's Crossing, Aladdin, 2001